Sarah's Child

Sarah's Child

Paul England
With Perry Gamsby

Sarah's Child

Published by Sarah's Child Press
A Division of Sunseal Garden Spas Pty Ltd
5 Lawson St, Southport, QLD 4215
'Sarah's Child' first published 2014
Www.facebook.com/sarahschildbook
Cover Art by P. Gamsby

ISBN 978-1500423278

Sarah's Child

Foreword

'Sarah's Child' is a work of fiction, but it is not a fairy tale. The events depicted in this novel are all too real. For millions of mothers, especially first-time mums, postpartum depression strikes and causes considerable damage. Damage to self esteem, to relationships, to lives.

'Sarah's Child' doesn't set out to vilify one side or another, but it does hope to draw attention to this condition and to the suffering of not only the mother, but everyone close to her. If by reading this novel you spend just a few minutes reading up on postpartum depression (PPD) then we have achieved one of our objectives. We have helped spread the word.

While many of the events fictionalized for this novel did happen in the lives of myself and my family, they have been transformed into what I trust is a very readable, very enjoyable work of fiction with the assistance of a professional writer. Perry Gamsby, D.Lit., M.A.(Writing), is an accomplished writer and published author whose own novels have been acclaimed as the epitome of 'Street Lit'. I chose Perry to assist me with this, my first novel, because while I knew the story I wanted to tell, telling it is not my strong suit. Leveraging the help of talented professionals like Perry is something all of us should do, particularly if we or someone we love is suffering as Sarah suffers in this story. There are several links to where such professional help can be obtained on our web site; **www.sarahschild.com.au**

Please enjoy 'Sarah's Child' as a work of fiction, but also as a call to action because mothers are a precious resource no society can afford to waste or allow to suffer.

Paul England,
Worcestershire, United Kingdom, 2014

Part One - Adam

In The Beginning…

"I've got just the young bloke you're after, Adam."

"Terrific, what's his name?"

"Stewart Lethbridge. He's my partner's son. Nathan's boy."

I hadn't met Nathan at this stage but Marg spoke so highly of him and she had helped me hire the now nearly two hundred people I had needed, usually in a hurry as the business grew, why wouldn't I trust her judgment? Well, the business didn't just grow, it bloody exploded! The Rudd government had decided to stimulate the economy with a scheme to put rain tanks in the garden and solar panels on the roof of every house in Australia, for free… O.K., at tax payer's expense, and we just couldn't keep up with the demand. If it hadn't been for Marg, we'd have missed out on getting the tender paperwork in and meeting the criteria you had to meet, such as it was, to get the work. Work that was pretty much like writing a blank cheque and getting the government to pay it every month.

"Alright, send him round, I'll give him a start with Geoff on the Southside tomorrow. Geoff'll show him the ropes." Geoff was one of my longest serving employees, joined me way back when I first came to Brissie from the U.K. and started throwing built-in wardrobes together. He could show the young bloke the ropes and make sure he gave us a fair day's work. That's all I ask, really. A fair day's work for a fair day's pay, and I was paying them very fair. Fairer than the Award said I had to, but then I've always been like that. Look after your staff and your staff will look after you, that's what my old man taught me and he had started his own business the day after he was de-mobbed from the war.

"Thanks, Adam. He's a good lad, a lot like his dad. He just needs to find something solid, ya know?"

"No worries, Marg. Afterall, he's only humping tanks and slinging panels up to Geoff, what harm could he get up to, eh?" If only I knew how ironic that last bit would turn out to be but back then, five years ago, if you had told me what was coming down the garden path to hit me like a freight train I would have told you to pull the other one. We had been doing well enough making and fitting built-in wardrobes, shower screens and doing patios. Had half a dozen or so working the factory, another half a dozen on the road installing and a full time sales manager, two girls in the office, if you count Sue, my wife; yeah, we'd been travelling pretty sweet. Then the global financial crises hit us like a ton of bricks and hit everyone with a mortgage just as hard. Nobody had any money to renovate or improve their homes, everyone was working too bloody hard just trying to hang on to the thing as it was. We had our own mortgage to watch the interest rate go up on, every month it seemed to get higher and higher. What made it worse was we still had a place in the U.K. and that we had to pay in pounds. Sterling. Real money! On top of the two mortgages we had the business. The factory rent, the wages, the materials and all the overhead and everyone wanted to be paid, didn't they?

Just as the work dropped to the point where the half a dozen or so people we had been able to keep on were thinking of slinging their hooks themselves, along comes the Stimulus Package and the great idea to make every private home eco-friendly. No cost to the home owner and it didn't take a genius to figure out how to follow the instructions on the pack. We never had any problems like those doing insulation had with batts being laid over down lights and setting the whole house on fire, or people electrocuting themselves by nailing the insulation to a live wire, although, sad to say, there were tragedies. But not in my firm. That's because I was very careful who I hired, even if we were screaming for people. That's why when one of your most trusted employees and, I suppose it's true to say at the time, a family friend, suggests their step-son, well why not? When he was installing he was alright, no problems, did the job, that kind of thing. It was only when he fell off the ladder and I put him to work in the warehouse on the fork that he gave any inkling of not being everything Marg said he was. Even then it wasn't anything you could give him his marching orders over, and when him and our Sarah started going out, well what can you do?

Sarah's my daughter. She's the dead spit of her mum and just as big hearted. I admit she's not the sharpest tool in the shed academically, as they say, but my boy Ethan, her older brother, he has all the brains and none of the common sense our Sarah has. Or had. I suppose given she was only nineteen then, working in the office with Sue and Marg and just a year younger than Stewart, so the pair of them were the only two under forty in the factory, it's no surprise they hit it off. Even before he went on light duties, Stewart was always keen to run back to the factory for more tanks and panels and always seemed to time it just around smoko or lunch so he could take his break with Sarah. He was a good enough looking lad, a little on the thickset side but then Sarah is a solid girl for her age, too. They hit it off straight away and I guess Sarah enjoyed the attention. At school she had always been conscious of being a little overweight and no doubt the other kids had teased her, helped her become shy and retiring to a degree. She was still pretty much the wall flower type when she started working with Sue and I in the factory, just a few hours a week at first while she did book keeping at TAFE. We'd wanted her to go on and do accounting at uni but she wasn't interested and you can't force your kids to study if they don't want to. You can't put an old head on young shoulders, as the old saying goes. Another old saying is there's no fool like an old fool and I think Stewart fooled us all. I'm not old, I was in my mid-forties then and the way things were going, Sue and I were looking at being able to retire very comfortably by the time I hit fifty. But then there's that other old saying, you know the one. The one about the best laid plans of mice and men going astray. Mine went off the bleeding rails.

IVF

There is something about a successful business that just breeds optimism. Mine was going along like a freight train full of houses on fire. I know that's a mixed metaphor but really, everything was just brilliant. I couldn't ask for any better, especially after the dark days of the GFC. We were raking it in. Working hard for it, but earning the rewards that come from hard work and a pretty sure thing. Solar panels were popping up on every roof in Brisbane and even more down the Gold Coast. We were proud we were able to employ so many people and help them live their dreams, too. I had one eye on the bubble though, because this was a bubble, blown into ginormous size by the government's stimulus package programs and like any bubble, one day it would burst. I wanted to be ready for that and so we looked at how we could sustain our income, and everyone else's that worked for us, once things got back to a more normal pace.

At that moment, though, I was thinking other thoughts, and I have to admit as far as what I had in mind back then for our future has worked out, I couldn't be happier. We were having coffee on the verandah one sunny winter's day, thinking about how if it were winter back in the UK we'd be inside with the central heating adding to the greenhouse gas footprint, or whatever they add to. Instead, we were soaking up the sun's warmth and just enjoying the moment.

"Sue. I've been thinking."

"That's dangerous, love" she laughed. I laughed back because I realised I had sounded pretty serious, but then what I was thinking wasn't something you decide to do lightly. "What've you been thinking, Adam?"

"We should have another baby."

I'll say this for our Sue, she can take it on the chin. No open mouthed stare, no wild reaction, no hesitation. Just came right back with, "a baby? What, adopt you mean?"

"No, I…"

"Foster parenting? One of the installer's does that. Him and his wife have three kids they are the carers for…"

"No, I mean we have another baby. Our own. A little brother or sister for Ethan and Sarah."

Sue thought about this for several seconds, although to me it seemed like minutes. I was the first to speak. "I thought we could, well, things are going great for us and we loved bringing up the kids and…"

"I know love. I'm not against the idea of another child, just…" Sue was still as beautiful in my eyes as the first time I saw her, but that was nearly a quarter of a century ago. I mean women have body clocks that stop ticking eventually, even if us blokes can still provide the ways and means, if you know what I'm saying.

"We can afford it…"

"It's not that, love. Of course we can afford it. Heck, we didn't have two bob to rub together when Ethan was born, or Sarah. We got by, they never went without. It's not the money, love, it's…"

"What?"

"Well. Aren't I too old? And what about you? I don't mean to be rude, love, but…" She went on without waiting for me to answer because it was obviously a rhetorical question. "I know how old I am and I know how old you are, too. You might be up for it but my body clock needs rewinding, maybe a new spring or two!"

"IVF."

"In vitero…"

"In Vitero Fertilization. They take an egg of yours and fertilize it with my sperm outside the womb. In a test tube. A test tube baby."

"Nobody calls it test tube baby anymore, Adam. IVF is how it's done for so many couples these days, but not couples well past forty." Well, not in Australia they don't but I had that covered. I figured I would ease into this bit, let Sue get a little more used to the idea of having another child.

"Yeah, true. Let's face it, our Sarah is as old as you were when you had Ethan, almost anyway. She could easily have her first child any day and that would make me a granddad."

"Hardly any day, pet! It takes a bit longer than that!"

We both laughed together, almost on cue. We'd been laughing with each other, and sometimes at each other, but in the best of ways, for so long now it was just something we did, it was how we were, are. How we are today but to be truthful, perhaps we don't laugh as often as we did then.

"Well c'mon then" she said.

"What do you mean 'c'mon then'?"

"Adam Clarkson, husband of mine, I have known you all my adult life and I know if you say you've been thinking, and it is about something as life changing as this, then you have done a lot of thinking and you've got it all sorted. Cough up!"

Sue smiled that smile she shares with me when she knows I'm still wrapped around that little finger of hers. Only because I want to be wrapped around it. Our marriage has had its ups and downs like everybody's, but we've always stuck it out and muddled through and neither of us would want it any other way. I know my Sue just as she knows me. She knows if I have been thinking about this then I have researched everything about this IVF idea. She's never one to go off half-cocked, that's my job. I'm the one that sees an opportunity and then leaps in with both feet and bugger the consequences. We'll deal with them when they show up. But I do my research, my due diligence as they say.

"Well, there is little to no chance anyone in Australia will do it. The IVF program here is very strictly regulated and women over 45 are almost never accepted into the program."

"What about back home?" she interrupted. The UK was still 'home' to us, even after living in Brisbane for nearly ten years at that time.

"Forget it, just as strict, if not stricter. We need to look a bit further afield."

"Well I'm not having it done in some third world place like India or Thailand. Remember Shelly from next door? Remember what happened to her left…"

"That was just bad luck. Could have happened to anyone."

"Couldn't have happened to a more deserving left…"

"Sue!"

We were both laughing again, thinking of our previous neighbour, Shelly. 'Smelly Shelly' I always called her. Not because she actually smelled or anything, just it rhymed and she was always poking her nose into everybody else's business. For months Shelly had talked of nothing but having her boobs done, a breast augmentation procedure she called it, in Thailand. Off she'd gone to some clinic in Phuket, a package holiday for two weeks including the boob job and time to convalesce in a five star resort, do lots of shopping then come home with the new puppies all nice and tanned. She couldn't wait to show them off, literally. We had her over for a pool party BBQ and she asked if she could swim topless. Sue was as curious as I was to see what ten grand in Thailand bought you so she said go ahead. Next thing Shelly whips off her bikini top and out comes two very large silicone boobs; one somewhat noticeably larger than the other. We couldn't help noticing and she couldn't help noticing our noticing and so she said one was still a bit swollen, they'd even out in a few weeks.

Well they never did. It was pretty tragic really. After a few months she went back to Thailand. I told Sue they must have a warranty clause but we never saw her again. Next thing her house is on the market, Phil, her partner, told us he was going off to FIFO work in the mines and they were splitting up. I didn't think Sue's IVF going tits up, pardon the pun, would split us up but I wasn't having her go anywhere cut rate and I said as much.

"Well they do it in Eastern Europe, Bulgaria, Romania and the Ukraine."

"No bloody way, love!" She was adamant. I know there are nice people in those countries and they have modern medical facilities but she just didn't trust them and to be honest, neither did I. Sue knew I would veto those places. I think she played me like an old violin but then she's always known how to get me to do what she wants. I know it's happening and all that and quite frankly, I like it. I love this woman and I'd die for her, literally I would and I trust her two hundred percent, so I don't mind being managed. I spend all my working day managing everybody else, sometimes it's just nice to sit back and be told, you know what I mean? "So where then? Where'd you find to do it?

"Cyprus, pet. There's a clinic in Northern Cyprus, the Turkish side. It's run by a couple of Brits with British trained locals for nurses and staff. All EU certified and accredited. Just they don't have to comply with EU regulations on age because they're not in the EU yet and they are happy to take the money from women over 45."

"I've always wanted to go to Cyprus, love" was all she said and she gave me that smile. The one she keeps for the most special of special occasions, the one I live every day for. Now I'm sounding like some soppy twit but I really do love that woman and I so wanted to make her happy. And we were. Are. Mostly.

Off To Cyprus

"You travelling overseas again?"

To be honest, I didn't like the tone Marg used, especially with the last word. What is it of her business how many times we travel, or where to? She is my employee. I admit she had become something of a family friend too but as the old saying goes, familiarity breeds contempt. Or maybe I was just a little touchy. We told everyone we were going to the UK, no mention of Cyprus or the IVF program. Why should we? It was nobody's business but our own. We hadn't even told Sarah at that stage, and telling Ethan would be a waste of breath.

"Yes. To the UK. Again." I might have added a little more emphasis to my last word than was necessary but I was a bit stressed at the time. I had orders to take care of for half a dozen customers who had called just that morning following our ad appearing in the local paper of the suburbs we were targeting this month. A good response and there would be more flooding in through the day and over the next two or three days until the newspaper was used to line garbage bins or whatever people did with them these days. "Sue and I need a break and we have family who are forever moaning about not seeing us, so…" I left the rest unsaid. Why should I feel this irrational need to explain myself, even defend my decisions to Marg?

"I didn't mean to upset you, Adam. I'm sorry if I…" she began, all soft and cushy. I felt a heel and tried to soften my own response.

"Nah, sorry Marg, I didn't mean to snap. Just a bit stressed, you know?" Why was I apologizing to her? I know why. Marg is that kind of person. You can't help but not want to upset her. She really does do so much for us and this business would suffer if she left. It wouldn't fall apart, I wouldn't let it. neither would Sue but I had to admit Marg was something of a godsend when the pace picked up. Like it had this morning. I quickly changed the topic.

" Anyway, while we are away I need someone to look after the two villas. Do you know anyone? Just a bit of cleaning and regular maintenance, keep the lawns under control, make sure the places are clean, fresh linen and all that?" Sue and I had two holiday homes, little villas side by side in a complex of ten with a shared pool and BBQ area. Right across from the beach. They made us a nice little fortune every school holidays but the rest of the year tenancy was sporadic to say the least. We had taken over managing them ourselves after three agents in a row rented them out to roughies. The last lot must have been conducting on-the-job training for demolition workers, the amount of damage they caused. We decided we could do just as bad a job and more likely a better one so I whipped up a web site, listed the villas with the usual online accommodation agents and we haven't looked back. Fewer out of season renters but no trouble.

"I could do that for you, Adam. Me and my partner, Nathan. You know, Stewart' dad?"

"Would you? That would be great. I'd pay you the same rates I paid the last contractor." The last contractor had died on the job humping a carpet steamer up fourteen flights of stairs to a holiday flat in a high-rise. The lift had an 'Out of Service' sign on the call button and being a conscientious contractor, he decided to use the stairs rather than come back another day. Turns out he had a dickey ticker. He was only 55, not much older than me. What was worse was the sign was a prank, played by some schoolies renting another unit. It made me think of all the 'what ifs?' What if the contractor, Arjanj his name was, a nice Iranian migrant fella, hadn't been so conscientious? What if the sign had fallen down and he had taken the lift? What if the renter had stayed an extra day or the next renter wasn't coming in for another week? Lots of what ifs.

"What if I get Nathan to come to the factory so you can meet him. He's a good worker, has his own lawn mower and you know I can clean like a pro." I almost laughed out lout at the mention of the word 'pro'. Marg had been a working girl for many years in her youth, then a decade or more as a 'madam' managing brothels all along the Gold Coast. She might have been worth the money in her day but a bit past her use by date now for my tastes, not that I played around on Sue or anything. Had plenty of opportunity, especially working away from home over the years, but I just figured I wouldn't like her doing it to me. You know what I mean?

"If you like, but not necessary, Marg. If you say he can do a good job then that's good enough for me. Hell, I'm leaving the business pretty much in your hands while we're gone so I should be able to trust your judgment, right?" And that was how I felt in those days. I really did trust Marg to take good care of our business. I paid her well. Well above the Award and with more than enough perks to keep her from looking somewhere else for a job. A lot of employers have the wrong attitude to their staff. They are vital to the business, otherwise why employ them. If you can get away with not hiring anyone you would, so anyone you hire has to be important, and if they are important then treat them accordingly. I don't mean fawn over them but look after them, keep them happy and content and they will work for you willingly and well. Well, that's the theory. Sadly I have learnt at great expense that some people tend to take things for granted; the nicer you are to them, the more they figure they can take you for a fool. Still, overall, on average it works for me and we tend not to have the not inconsiderable expense of recruiting and retraining new staff on a regular basis. I wanted someone I felt I could trust looking after the villas as we'd be away for a school holiday month and we had bookings, one was a repeat customer so we wanted to make sure they really loved the place all over again and told their friends. It's how it works and it works like a charm, nothing like word of mouth referrals but one little upset can turn the word of mouth into a slagging off that hurts your bottom line. I felt confident Marg and Nathan would do a good job and we'd come back in three months to everything running as smoothly then as it was now. If only…

"No worries, Adam. I'll get the details off you later. Meanwhile we have this four panel in Logan, the owner wants it on the shady side of the roof so it can't be seen from the street!"

***

"They said we'd be met at the arrival hall by their driver. Oh look! There must be a dozen drivers there, all holding up signs with people's names on them." Sue was a little tense but perhaps it was just the late hour? Our flight from Manchester had been delayed for five hours and instead of arriving in the early afternoon it was now dark and past our dinner time.

"Well, read them and see if any have our name on it" I said, a bit of stating the bleeding obvious never hurt in these situations; just watch the tone. My tone must have been borderline because Sue gave me her 'don't you start' look and I made a mental note to ease up the sarcasm. Women often ask what blokes think are asinine, obvious questions when they are stressed or just giving the other person a chance to share their emotions with them. Us men think they actually want an answer that delivers a solution and the solution is usually so obvious, well we get sarcastic. But it's not about the solution. Women know the answer, they just like to share the love, or something. I know all this but I've been a bloke far longer than I have been aware of the Mars and Venus thing so I usually forget myself and come back with a typical blokey response and kick off a row that never needed to happen.

"Over there love, that bloke in the black leather jacket." I pointed with one of the suitcases at a swarthy chap wearing a black leather jacket, jeans and a green polo shirt. He had a piece of cardboard with 'Clarkson' in black felt tip pen written on it and he was looking around for anyone he figured looked like a Clarkson, I guess. I stepped ahead of Sue and called out to him, "you looking for Adam and Sue Clarkson? You from the clinic?" I almost said IVF clinic but caught myself just in time.

"Yes, sir. My name is Yanov, I am doctor driver. I come for you. Hello."

OK, so he spoke reasonable English, always a good sign. "Hello Yanov, my name is Adam, this is Sue." As soon as I introduced ourselves I realised I had just stated the bleeding obvious, too. Must be something in the air-conditioning here in the terminal. That's my excuse anyway.

"Yes, I know, it is on the sign. Please, let me help you with your bags, I have a trolley." He produced a luggage cart from behind himself and loaded our bags aboard, then set off for the car park exit without looking around. I looked back briefly after the third step to see the 'Clarkson' sign lying on the ground where he had dropped it while loading the cart. I felt this silly urge to pick it up and put it on the cart, or in the bin but while I dithered he and Sue were now almost at the exit doors. I took off after them and caught up as Yanov pushed the cart in front of a taxi that had just started to pull away from the kerb. He gave the cart a push with one hand, signaled to the cab driver something universally understood with the right, then used it to whip out a cigarette and lighter and set fire to the end.

"Car is at back of park. When I got here this afternoon very many cars parking."

"Yes, sorry, our flight was delayed…" Sue tried to offer.

"I know. I stood there long time then announcement came so I went for coffee. No problem you here now. We go."

It was all very matter of fact and to be honest, like something out of a spy movie. You know, where the secret agent is met by the quirky local contact with the forced accent and too funny simplified English. Only this was happening for real and we weren't secret agents. Maybe not secret agents but our mission was pretty secret. We had told nobody, not a soul. Just in case it all fell through. We knew we were going to raise eyebrows and cause tongues to wag so why give them any longer than necessary and if it didn't take then why give them anything to gossip about at all?

"Here is car. Get in."

It was a ute, or a pickup as our American cousins would call it. It had a dual cab so there was a front seat and a back seat, both of which held Yanov's possessions including a recyclable shopping bag, an umbrella, two plastic bags with maybe magazines or news papers in them and a selection of fast food containers, empty for the most part. Yanov put our bags in the tray, open to the elements and no doubt any passers by who might help themselves at the traffic lights. I'd seen that happen to a ute in front of us on holiday in Thailand once. Some street vendor kid distracts the driver by trying to sell them bottles of water or single cigarettes while his friends rush up and clean out the tray. They time it just as the lights go green so the traffic starts hitting the horns and the driver is stuck between a fruitless chase on foot or simply taking the hit and driving off.

"Is this it? The doctor has you drive him around in this?"

"No. He has a Range Rover but no good to get through the border. They see flash British car they keep you there all day, maybe strip it apart."

"Is that the Turkish side?"

"No. Turkish side all cool. It is the Greek side, South Cyprus that is the problem. Ever since they made it into EU they think they special, give hard time to people from North Cyprus."

I confess the three hour drive would have been far more comfortable in a posh Range Rover, but at least we weren't fighting the crowds on a public bus. As we pulled out of the car park I looked over to the lines of people waiting to board the two coaches standing at the kerb and it looked like organized chaos. Maybe not too organized. The bus took longer because at the border they checked every passenger, plus the driver, plus the vehicle, and often delayed things with unnecessary luggage searches. Yanov explained this to us as we drove away from the airport and into a very dark night.

He certainly knew the road north, or at least I hoped he did given the speed he took the corners and how many times he swerved to miss the potholes. This wasn't a road as such, merely a series of various size and depth holes joined together by a thin veneer of asphalt. As we wound our way into the mountains the swerving and twisting increased almost to brown paper bag proportions but both Sue and I managed to keep it together. As cliché as it sounds, just as we both felt we had suffered enough torment and could we please stop for a break, we reached the border.

The border guards and customs officials were sour faced, but by now it was after midnight and no one dealing with the general public is at their cheery best this time of the night. They only asked us to open one bag, then they waved us through. The next checkpoint was a little better, at least they tried to be courteous but you could tell some of them had had a long, hard day.

So had we, so when an hour and a bit later we reached our hotel, we were ready to take whatever was coming, just so long as it had a bed and a lock on the door. Given the state of the ute and how, even though nighttime we could see the difference between the developed south and the more 'traditional' north, we weren't too surprised to find the hotel looking pretty average on the outside. Nothing fancy and not the kind of place you'd steal the linen from, but it was basic, clean and it seemed secure. The room had a safe, the same model I have seen in hotel rooms around the world. There was a clean en suite bathroom and the receptionist assured us the room service ran 24 hours if we needed anything. We said goodbye to Yanov, I didn't know if we were to tip him and if we did, how much? Did we add something for having to wait for our delayed flight? I just couldn't be asked to figure this out so I thanked him and asked him outright if we tipped him or not.

"Up to you, no pressure," was all he said and that was no help. I pulled out twenty euros and hoped that was enough.

"Yanov, hope this buys you a drink, thanks for getting us here safely."

"My pleasure and thank you for tips."

Yanov closed the door behind himself as he left and I slipped the chain in place, turned around and there was Sue, sitting on the bed, a look of relief and utter bewilderment on her face. I glanced at the large wall mirror behind the dresser and saw my own expression pretty much matched hers.

"Bugger me, pet! What a trip!"

"Yes, and we are due at the clinic in seven hours."

"Six. Different time zone. C'mon, let's get some sleep."

"Right after I have a shower. I feel like half the roadside dirt in Cyprus is clinging to me."

"I'll join you, I've got the other half stuck to my armpits."

"Adam Clarkson! Behave yourself. No funny business tonight… they can tell you know."

I was so shagged the only funny business I was up for was falling asleep to Michael McIntyre playing on the satellite TV. We'd been having our own comedy roadshow, just me, Sue and our mate Yanov!

Meanwhile, Back At The Ranch

They say ignorance is bliss and they are correct. It is, but once the ignorance is removed and you become aware of what has been going on in your absence, I think the effect is twice as devastating. While we were in the UK and Cyprus, the business had been left in the culpable hands (yes, I know what I just wrote) of our Office Manager, Marg. Sarah was there to represent the family and keep everyone honest, or at least make them think twice before robbing us blind. Of course if she hasn't a clue what's going on then she can't really do much to stop it and if she's being handled by someone as cunning and capable as Marg, there was little hope for the poor lamb.

Naturally, I knew nothing of this decline in the family fortunes while we were away. I pieced this all together only after we returned and some of it I only found out as recently as last week. The business was going along alright, the solar installations were booked for the next three months and more seemed to come in every day from the regular little ad I ran in several local newspapers. Rain tanks were a bit slow, but they are pretty seasonal and it wasn't the right season so I wasn't bothered. The problem was mine and Sue's little retirement project, the holiday flats. We were still in the UK and yet to fly out to Cyprus when I got the first inkling not all was well back home.

"So what are you saying, Marg?" I asked.

"Nathan was wondering when you would be paying his invoice. It is for the first two weeks of work and…"

"You know we always pay on thirty days, Marg. What's the…"

"I know, I told him that but he says he needs to be paid every fortnight, preferably the other fortnight, not this one."

"Other fortnight? What you talking about?"

"He gets his Centrelink next fortnight so he would like his pay this week. Helps him budget better."

I was stunned. "Do you mean to tell me he has been running his cleaning contract business for the last two weeks and all the time he is on Centrelink benefits?" I hadn't bothered to ask Marg if he was on the dole or anything, why would I? She had made out he had a business set up already, with an ABN and everything. I know you can get the Australian Business Number online, even if you aren't a business, but you can't run a business and collect unemployment benefits at the same time. "Is he, I mean, well what benefit is he on then?"

There was a pause before she replied. "It's NewStart, but for self-employed people. He's allowed to make some income, he just has to declare it and they adjust his benefit payments. It's all perfectly legal, Adam."

Her tone as she spat the last sentence down the phone didn't go unnoticed. I could tell she was miffed and I thought at the time fair enough. I won't tolerate people ripping off the system, it's there to protect people from hard times but too many abuse it. Apart from the legal risks of having a dole cheat working for me, I just don't like bludgers. I had jumped to conclusions and thought he was ripping off the government, claiming a benefit and working at the same time. I knew she was correct. If he was on NewStart as a self-employed person then he could still make money, so long as he declared it in his tax return and they would adjust future payments or make him pay any over payments back. Still, there was something I didn't like about this. I couldn't put my finger on what it was exactly but you know when something doesn't ring true.

"Sorry, Marg, I didn't mean to... Look, we pay all our bills on 30 days, or longer..."

"Yeah, but we pay the installers on seven. They slip us their invoice on the Friday arvo and I put the money into their account by the next..."

"I know how we pay them, Marg. I own the company, remember?" I confess my tone was a bit harsh now, but I didn't need the lecture on how my own business paid its people. "I hadn't thought of you and Nathan doing the flat cleaning as part of the business. I always paid Arjanj the first of the month following his invoice. Actually you and Sue paid him along with all the other accounts; that's why I thought..."

"No worries, Adam." Her voice was back to the soft, sweet Marg I was used to. "I shouldn't have been so..." She left it there. I normally caught up with her via Skype and we had a video call to keep me in the loop but I was on my way to the airport so I thought I'd just use up the last credit on my UK mobile. I wonder how the conversation would have run if we'd had video? You miss so much without the facial expressions and the body language, too easy to get the wrong impression and react differently than if you were face to face, even via a video link.

"Nah, sorry, Marg. Just flat out over here, you know?" We both toned it down and chatted about non-business matters for a minute or so. I told Marg to write Nathan a cheque for his invoice but she could cash it and pay him out of petty cash right away if he was short. I made a mental note to check his invoices when I got back, or maybe Marg could email them to me. Then I remembered she was his 'employee', or partner or whatever in that venture so better to get Sarah to do it. I don't know why I thought that. Just had the beginning of a niggle, I suppose.

An hour later Sue and I were told our plane was delayed so we wandered off looking for a place to watch the time go by and have a coffee and a bite. To be honest I totally forgot about the call after I had filled Sue in on the various events going on back at the factory. She didn't say anything then but later she admitted she's had a funny feeling about the whole Nathan and Marg flat cleaning thing from the very start. Sue was a bit canny like that, as my old granny used to say. You would think by now I'd have the sense to pay more attention when Sue says she has one of her 'twinges', but I was too pumped up about Cyprus, the IVF and everything else to pay much attention.

Good News… And Bad

"Wink in cup, pleez Meester Arrdarm" the nurse said. I looked at her, then at the plastic jar with the yellow screw-on cap. It was a standard, sterile specimen collection jar just like hundreds I had peed in over my lifetime. Well, dozens maybe. I took the jar and looked at it more closely. Then I winked at it like she had told me to.

"Ha ha, you very funny man. No wink," she winked at me, first the left eye, then the right, just so there was no confusion I presume. "You know, wink in cup!" and she did the hand actions to match so I was left in no doubt. She must have had some great stories to tell her girlfriends after her shifts in the fertility clinic.

"Oh! Wank! Yeah, I get it. Wank in the cup! Of course, you need a sample, I mean a specimen, yeah?"

She beamed with relief as the thick as a brick Brit client (that was me) finally realised what she wanted me to do. Sue was already in the operating room or insertion clinic or whatever they called it, getting her eggs 'harvested'. I wasn't sure what that entailed but I imagined it would be a tad more invasive than obtaining my contribution.

"Yes. Pleez go pee pee then go winky, OK?"

"Pee pee then winky…yeah, sure, my pleasure love."

The nurse, now she had both hands free, opened the door to the room where legends were made, so to speak, and gestured for me to squeeze past her and step inside. I was expecting, well I guess I don't really know what I was expecting but it wasn't what I got. I had imagined a room with a couch or bed of some kind, maybe posters on the wall of centerfold models, perhaps a few stick books, as we used to call porno mags, perhaps even a TV with a DVD player showing helpful instructional videos, if you get my drift. I certainly didn't expect a rather small and impersonal toilet cubicle. There was the toilet, a sink with a tap, soap dispenser, toilet paper holder, paper towels and a waste paper bin. That was it. Not even a mirror on the wall above the sink. For making sure your hair was combed, of course. When it came to setting the mood to make yourself a new heir and successor, it was severely lacking in any kind of appropriate stimulus and to be brutally frank, the wink in the cup nurse was about 20 years of doner kebabs past her prime, not meaning to be rude but just truthful. So I was rather bereft of recent imagery to assist!

I figured this was it so I better get on with the job in hand, so to speak and off I went, wrestling with the dilemma. It took a while I must say. I mean from zero to hero with no external stimulation and let's face it, I'm not some horny teenager pushing out a hard-on every time he sees a shop mannequin. It was hard work but I grasped the nettle and got on with it. The end result was, the doctor commented later, rather less than he had hoped for but I felt, under the circumstances, he was lucky to get as much as he did.

It took the best part of ten minutes, maybe longer but just as I was screwing on the cap of the jar, there was a polite tapping on the door and a muffled, "Meester Arrdarrm, you there?"

Feeling rather flushed with my success under such adverse conditions, I whipped open the door with a flourish and stepped out of the toilet holding the specimen jar aloft, discreetly wrapped in a paper towel. Feeling no need to be shy, after all we were among professionals, I proudly announced my successful sperm production.

"Job's done!"

It was at this point that I noticed the room itself. Strangely enough it seems now but, at the time I had followed the nurse to the room, my focus had been on the little jar with the yellow cap. The room was actually an open plan laboratory, a dozen desks each equipped with a microscope, computer terminal and a little specimen centrifuge filled the otherwise rather large space. I later learned this was also a pathology lab for the local region and the ten or twelve, mostly female, lab techs all looked up in muted surprise when I proudly announced my triumph of the human spirit. Or whatever it was.

So there I was, at the entrance to the lab's toilet, a yellow specimen jar of my finest wrigglers held up for all to see and the eyes of some ten or twelve bemused foreign lab techs all riveted on me. Almost on cue, they spontaneously applauded. I blushed, but I got into the spirit of the moment and did a bow, then a curtsey and then another bow before the applause faded away. As silence returned I turned, grinning like the Cheshire Cat at the winky nurse who merely turned on her heel and said over her shoulder; "Very good, but winking room is next door. That is just pees house to clean out chubes."

I now turned beetroot red as the entire lab broke into laughter. Either these people all understood English (which they did) or I wasn't the first client to rush the job. Perhaps the proud display of the jar, albeit discreetly wrapped in a paper towel, was the clincher for me. All I know as I staggered, dazed, into the 'Wink Room' was the super cute little lab tech at the desk right by the door looked up, smiled, winked and said, "those walls are very thin, but I don't mind." I confess by now I was glad I had already done my duty because there was no way I could have performed, despite the 'Wink Room' being fully equipped with every aid to arousal you can think of. The nurse simply relieved me of the jar and told me to wait here while she had it tested. I switched on the TV but there was nothing but porn on every channel. Flicking away with the remote, which I wiped, by the way, it looked like one reality TV hospital show after another, all doing close ups of open heart surgery. I was so glad when the door opened and Sue was standing there, gazing curiously around the rather erogenously decorated room.

"Very nice! You get to do it in here; me, I'm on a Gyno chair with me ankles tied behind my ears!"

I laughed and said, "This is where I was supposed to conceive but, er…"

"Yeah, I know. The nurse told the doctor and he even called up a colleague. You're famous!"

That was it. We just cracked up and we were still laughing when Yanov dropped us back at our hotel. Sue had to rest and do nothing for a few days. I was free to roam around but instead I chose to keep Sue company in the room until she ordered me to go for a walk and stop fussing over her. After a week, during which Sue had been allowed to get up and do more and more, we were ready to head back to the UK. We'd done the local markets to death and the night life wasn't much to write home about compared to other places nearby but then this town was chosen because it was quiet, peaceful and not full of raging night clubbers. Patients needed rest and relaxation for the fertilized egg to take.

The ride back to the airport was just as scary only now, in daylight, perhaps worse as we could see the precipitous drop on the one side and the sheer cliff to be pinned and crushed against on the other, every time a kamikaze truck or bus driver careered down the national goat track of a highway at us. Yanov was driving so smoothly and carefully it was clear he knew how important it was that the egg was not dislodged from the womb wall. I made a mental note to erase the mental note I'd made on the trip there and give him a decent tip when we got to the airport.

Yanov earned his fifty Euros and he was very pleased at his gratuity. It helped him remember he had been given a message for us at the hotel desk by the receptionist who was too shy to speak in English to her guests, even though she spoke it well. Instead she had seen Yanov with our bags and slipped him the message. Yanov forgot about it in the flurry of getting us into the car and heading off and it was only when he slipped his tip into his pocket that he found the message and remembered it was for us.

I thanked him and was about to open it and read what it said when Sue said, "C'mon, read that at the bar. I need a drink and so do you!"

We'd already checked in so we went to the bar, bought a ridiculously expensive white wine for Sue and a lager for me and pondered not for the first time why airports the world over charge so much? It's even worse in countries like this where away from the airport the beer and wine are very cheap, due to little tax and, away from the tourist areas, they are virtually free. But sell them at an airport and you have a license to gouge.

After half of the beer had done its job I remembered the message and pulled it out of my pocket, by now quite crumpled and looking like just another unwanted receipt or slip of paper we all accumulate in our wallets, pockets and bags. I smoothed it out on the bar top and read it. Twice. Then I read it a third time and then I said one word… "F…"

"Love?" Sue was looking at me with her head to one side as I scrabbled for my cell phone. I punched in the +, the 6, the 1, then the numbers for Sarah's mobile back home and there was nothing. Not even a voice message or something recorded by the phone people. Nothing. I stabbed in the quick dial number for the office and it took forever to connect, then it just rang. It rang out and I looked at my watch. It was ten in the morning here, it would be past closing time there. I was using my address book in the phone memory when Sue grabbed my arm and dug her fingers in like claws and shook me like a rag doll!

"Adam! What the hell's the matter!"

I just looked at her and nearly burst into tears. I'm no softie but I am not ashamed to say I love my wife, my kids and if anything ever happened to any of them, anything like this, I'd be devastated. I was on the verge of devastation right then and there but I knew I had to keep it together. For Sue's sake as much as my own. Losing it now would achieve nothing. We were two airports away from a flight to where we had to be right then and there, and getting there as quickly as possible was going to take some managing.

"Adam! For fuck's sake…"

Hearing Sue swear brought me back to the here and now. She rarely lets the bad ones loose but she must have been very worried to do it here. Then I caught sight of her face and I realised she was not just worried, she was terrified. Terrified because she knew that what I had read in the message had clicked me into survival mode, something she had never seen before. But she knew, she just knew. She was a mother and she was sharp and she put two and two together faster than you could read the eleven words of the message:

'Marg killed Sarah Stewart in car crash, come home back ok?'

Part Two - Sue

Killed, Culled, Called

"Adam, what are we going to do?" I was desperate to say the least. I thought this was the worst moment of my life. I had just been given the fertilized egg that would become our third child, our third beautiful child and I had never felt happier. It might have been Adam's idea to have a baby again after so many years but I wanted one too, just as much. Perhaps even more. Being a mother is something nearly every woman wants, it defines her as a woman, as corny as that sounds, but it does. Looking back now, that moment Adam handed me the message was not the worst moment of my life because that was still to come, but at the time it certainly did the job.

"We need to call home, make sure, I mean... Christ!"

Adam was as beside himself as I was. He didn't panic though, not on the outside, but I know my Adam. Inside he would be feeling as sick and helpless as I was. I just let my feelings show more than he does.

"Get on your phone, call Sarah, call..."

"Love, I am almost out of battery and I don't have much load left on my local SIM. It's night time there, nobody is at the office, I don't know who to..."

"Call the police! Call the hospital!"

"Which bloody hospital? Which police station? Christ Sue!" he snarled at me. I hadn't seen him so angry and upset before, not once in all the years I had known him. I physically shrunk back, he was that livid. "Sue! I'm sorry, I didn't mean to snap at you, I'm just..."

"I know love, I know." He wasn't angry at me, just at the helplessness of it all. We were stuck here about to board a plane with no way of knowing if our daughter was alive or dead, just a scribbled note from the hotel receptionist telling us unbelievable news. But then you never want to believe something like this, do you? We go into denial and try and fool ourselves it's not real, not true, but people do die. People do kill other people, but Marg? Killing Sarah and Stewart? Whatever could have made her do such a thing? Marg was a family friend, she worked for us, we trusted her with our business.

"No love, there's no way Marg killed Sarah and Stewart, not on purpose. It says in a car accident. Maybe it means she was driving the car?" I offered.

"So why was she driving them? Sarah has her own car, so does Stewart, I don't understand why she would be driving them anywhere."

We exchanged a few ideas as to why Marg might have been giving them a lift somewhere but none of this was getting us anywhere close to knowing what had happened, what was happening now, the outcome. The truth.

"I'll call the hotel, ask to speak to the receptionist who took the message and see if that clarifies things. Meanwhile we better head for the gate, they just announced boarding."

I'd missed the announcement, I was so focussed on thinking about Sarah and Marg and Stewart and all the 'what ifs'. We began walking to the gate, our carry-on suitcases on wheels following behind us just like Sarah and Ethan had when they were little. I had a silly moment where I imagined my bag would run ahead and turn around, laugh and then run even further with me calling it back, warning it not to get too far ahead or we'd lose it in the crowd. We'd lost Sarah just that way once. It was in Marks and Spencer's, back in the UK. Sarah was three and full of beans. She just disappeared in the crowd. One second she was just ten or twelve feet in front and then she was not there. I had rushed ahead, frantically searching the legs of the crowd for her little mischievous face grinning up at me but there was nothing. I had a black cloud come over me, I was sick to my stomach with worry. Then there was a tug on my skirt and she was there, giggling and laughing and I nearly smothered her with my hug, then scolded her for scaring me to death, and then I hugged her again. Only a parent knows how that feels, that confusion of love and anger and relief and desperation.

"Yes, the receptionist, the younger one. Front desk. Could you put her on the phone, please?" Adam was through to the hotel and asking for the woman who took the message. "This morning you gave me a message… Yes, Adam Clarkson. Room 204. Yes, Sue Clarkson. This morning, you… Yes, no, I need to know what the message said, who was it from… no I have the message here, in my hand… yes, but no, I need to know… Look, let me read it to you…"

Adam was doing his best to keep his voice calm and under control but I could see he was struggling. He was doing a better job than I would have; I would have been hysterical and while I know that would only make things worse, I can't help it. That's why Adam was calling. As clichéd as it sounds, he is my rock. And I am his sea bed as he likes to reply. We do make a good couple, have done ever since we first met. I think it is because we are good at different things and complement each other. There's no power struggle between us. He's the Lord and Master and I'm the Boss, ha ha. That's what Adam always says. We reached the gate lounge and stopped so Adam could keep talking to the hotel receptionist. They make you turn your phones off when you go into the gate lounge these days and this was a conversation we had to complete.

"So it was Marg who called? Marg Jones? She called and said Sarah and Stewart... hello? Hello? Oh shit!"

"Love?"

"Bloody phone died. Battery! Bugger!"

"What did she say?"

"She said the call was from Marg in Australia and that Sarah and Stewart had been in a car accident that morning. I asked her if she had written down the message on another pad, which she didn't understand, but she said she remembered it clearly as it was the only message she has written today and it was from Australia and all that but then the phone died."

"So Marg was the caller, she sent the message?" I asked.

"Yes. She said Sarah and Stewart had been in a car accident that morning and..."

"Adam! If Marg was calling then I seriously doubt she had been driving the car." I had just had one of those epiphany things they go on about. A moment of clarity where suddenly I had figured it out.

"What do you mean, love?"

"Think about it. If you were driving a car, well not you, say me, if I were driving the car that was in an accident and my passengers were killed, do you really think I would be in any fit shape to call their parents a few hours later?" I know I would be a wreck, wouldn't you? I would be under sedation and in no fit state to call anyone, let alone make an international call to my dead passenger's parents, friends of mine no less.

Adam thought this through, I know the face he uses when he is thinking, calculating, figuring out the odds and the angles as he says, and he had this face on at that moment. It was a better face to look at than the one he'd been wearing up till now. The worried sick, can't do anything, totally helpless parent face. I'd never seen that face before that day but I was going to see it a lot in the months to come, I just didn't know it at the time.

"So you're saying Marg wasn't driving the car?"

"Yes."

"So it wasn't Marg that killed them?"

"Adam, they're not dead. They were in a car accident, doesn't mean they were killed. Did the receptionist say that?"

"That they were killed?"

"Yes, no. I mean did she say Marg killed them? Like what's written in the message?"

"No, she said 'a person called Marg called. Sarah and Stewart in car crash...' "

"A person called Marg called? Not killed? Show me the note again."

Adam pulled the note out from his shirt pocket where he'd stuffed it and I virtually snatched it out of his hand. "There! See! Look! The way she has written 'killed'. It could be 'called'. See how the 'k' and the 'i' could be a 'c' and an 'a'?"

Adam just about snatched the note back and scrutinised it, turning it sideways and back. "Yes! Sue you are a genius! All those nights keeping me up reading those detective mysteries in bed! You are a bloody Sherlock Holmes!" I like to read just before going to sleep and when I'm not reading a romance mystery, it's a crime mystery. I've read all the usual stuff, the classics like Agatha Christie and the rest. You just pick stuff up and never know when it might be useful. I'd been reading mysteries and 'whodunit's since I was a girl. I guess you could say I've spent 40 years of my life training to be a detective and all that reading was paying off here in the airport terminal gate lounge!

"So, if the message now reads, 'Marg called Sarah and Stewart in car crash come home back ok', at least they aren't dead!"

You know that line they use in books about how a 'wave of relief washed over me'? Well it really does. This was not a wave though, it was a bloody huge dumper! Not for a moment did either of us think we had it wrong. This made perfect sense. As we boarded the plane and took our seats we discussed the message and the girl who took it.

"Yeah, I mean when I spoke to her she seemed perfectly calm, like there was nothing wrong. You'd think if she was passing on news of a tragedy she would have the common sense to tell us in person..."

"To make the effort to let us know directly, not by a note like that..."

"Exactly. These are decent people, they're not cold, callous robots without feelings. No way would that girl tell us our daughter is dead with just a scribbled note..."

Which all made perfect sense. We decided that if there was a mix-up with 'killed' and 'called', there might be something else in the message that wasn't quite right, too. By the time the plane landed in Manchester we had decided to stay up late and call the office as soon as it opened in the morning, about 7a.m. Brisbane time. We'd talk to Marg and get the real story. Both of us were certain now that whatever had happened wouldn't be as dire as we had first thought and that everything would be ok. I have to say I was relieved, not just for Sarah and Stewart, who we were sure were both alive and if not completely well, at least in good hands and on the mend, but for our new addition to the family. The first two weeks are critical for the egg to take hold and do its thing. All sorts of things could put the 'kybosh', as my dad used to say, on the pregnancy and make it never happen. Shock did horrible things to the body and I could only hope that the shock I had experienced when Adam first gave me the note was not enough to harm our new baby. It gave me more than a few moments of quiet reflection on the trip back to our home on the outskirts of Manchester.

No News Is Good News

Many mothers will tell you, you know when your child is in trouble. Somehow, you just know. Maybe not every mother or every time something happens in your child's life, but some just have that sixth sense. I have it and my mother had it, and she told me granny was the same. A few hundred years ago they used to burn women like us at the stake, called us witches, but it really is just something natural some of us have. Perhaps at one time all women had this gift but over the generations it has faded away. Whatever the way things are, I just knew Sarah wasn't dead. I didn't know if she was hurt or anything, I just knew she was still alive. And I was right.

"I'll call again, somebody has to be there by now. Marg's not answering her mobile and her home number just had her answering machine. I left a message on the one at work so…" Adam was working the phone, systematically calling various numbers back in Australia, just hoping someone would have some news. So far our neighbour had said he last saw Sarah two days ago but he'd let us know if he learned anything and Geoff said he was on a job and had the new lad with him, Stewart had called in sick or something. He didn't know the details, got them third hand apparently. None of which was helping but as they say, no news is good news.

"Hello? Marg? Oh, Mahmed, it's Adam, I'm calling from the UK, who's in the office there?"

Mahmed was one of our employees, a nice man, immigrated from Egypt a few years ago. A top little worker according to Adam but his English wasn't the best, as I could hear from Adam's side of the conversation.

"No, Marg sent a message to us, yes, said Sarah and Stewart…" Mahmed must have said something because Adam stopped talking and just listened. "Yeah. OK. OK. Yeah. No. Thanks, talk to you later, cheers."

"Well?"

"Well Marg is at the hospital. She asked Mahmed to pop by her place and pick up the key to the office and open up the factory so the…"

"What about Sarah?" I didn't need a blow by blow description of how the business was being kept going in our absence, I needed to know if my daughter was still alive! Men, I tell you. You love them dearly but sometimes…

"*As* I was saying, pet. Marg is at the hospital, probably why her mobile is turned off, you can't have them…"

"Get on with it Adam!"

"He says Sarah and Stewart were in a car accident and they are in hospital but not serious as far as he knows. Then again, he might have it wrong, you know how he got the Housing Commission tender…"

"Forget bloody work for a minute, Adam. What do we know about Sarah? Which hospital is she in?"

"Bugger! I forgot to ask. I'll call him back." It was like a movie or something. Right on cue, as soon as he said he would call him back, the phone rang. It was Mahmed.

"Yes, mate. OK. OK. OK. Great, champion, thanks!" and he hung up.

"Mahmed?"

"Yeah, he said sorry, he forgot to tell us the hospital and give us the phone number."

"Which hospital? What's the number?"

"Hold on, he's sending it by text." We both looked at the mobile phone in Adam's hand and again, as if on cure, the text message signal sounded and the hospital name and number appeared on the screen. Adam swiped the screen, hit the messages icon then pressed the message to kick start the call. Nothing happened.

"Must be the wrong number, Adam." He had hit the speaker button so I could hear there was nothing happening. No ring tone or anything. I grabbed the phone and twisted it so I could check if there was a signal. It was as strong as it gets so that couldn't be the problem. Adam tried the number again, taking his time and making sure he did everything properly. Same result. Nothing. "Adam, ring him back, check the…" but he was way ahead of me and already selecting the redial option for the office.

"Of course! No bloody wonder, Sue!"

He was almost laughing as he started stabbing at the screen. "What you doing, love?"

"International prefix! You know like when you ring your mum you have to get an international line first, then the country code and so on. Mahmed just sent me the local number. I have to add a + and a 61 for Oz and a 7 for Brissie."

This time the call went through and in seconds Adam was explaining to the receptionist who we were and who we were after. There was a further delay of five hours that I know they will swear was only five seconds, but by now I was almost beside myself. Everything was ticking by so slowly, my senses were so alert but funny thing, all I could see was the phone in Adam's hand. It was as if everything else in the room had blurred and I had tunnel vision.

"Yes, Clarkson, Sarah Clarkson, she's... She is? Great! Thanks, please." He covered the phone with his other hand and smiled at me, "they're putting us through to her room now. To her, she said. Sarah."

I grabbed his wrist and gripped it like a python! My head was next to his, even though the speaker meant I could have been across the room and still heard every word, but I was so tense as you can imagine.

"Hello?" That was Sarah! I knew it! I knew she wasn't dead. She sounded tired but fine.

"Sarah, it's your da..." I snatched the phone away from Adam. I know, it was on speaker but I exercised my inalienable mothering rights!

"Sarah, love, are you alright? How are you? What happened, love? Are you OK? Is Stewart Ok? Is he there with you? Are you..."

"Mum! MUM! I'm fine, OK." Sarah was laughing. You can not believe how good it was to hear her laugh. "One question at a time, Mum! I'm OK. Stewart is OK. We were hit from behind while we were stopped at the lights, you know the ones near work where Dad always says to..."

"Oh Sarah, I am so relieved to hear your voice. We were told you were..." Something made me stop. I didn't want to say it. I didn't want to remember how it felt just a few hours ago back at the airport in Cyprus.

"Ah, Mum, we're fine. It was horrible though. As I said, this ute hit us from behind. The driver was on his mobile, texting someone and he just forgot to stop! Hit us ever so hard. I have a sore neck and Stewart has a sore neck and chest from hitting the steering wheel. Bloody airbags didn't go off. Apparently that model they only go off if you hit something in front of you."

"We'll get you a new car, love, one with hundreds of airbags." Adam was grinning like the proverbial Cheshire Cat. I had a thought right at that moment; Sarah was his child, too. He loved her as much as I did, even if he loved her as a father and of course, me as her mother. I don't know if men love their kids differently or for different reasons, I can only speak for mothers really, and then only for myself. But I know he loves her so much he would have switched places with her in a heartbeat if he could. Even if it had meant his own death. I know I'd do it. It sounds a bit melodramatic but it's true. You give them life and yet you can't live their lives for them, nor can you protect them from everything life has to throw at them, but you would if you could.

"I just want to go home now, Dad. Sleep for a week and forget this ever happened."

"I know love. When will they let you go home?"

"Today. Doctor's doing his rounds in half an hour. Marg was here, just left. She said to give her a ring when we get the OK and she'll give us a lift home. Stewart should be let go, too. He's on the loo, we got a room just for the two of us, dead posh it is."

Adam and I laughed together as Sarah said that. We might have a few bob, thanks to hard graft, but we're still working class at heart and proud of it. We earned every penny and thankfully our Sarah hasn't grown up spoiled or anything. We chatted for another ten minutes until the nurse told Sarah she had to hang up as the doctor was on his way and what have you. We let Sarah hang up first, both of us not wanting to break the connection first. I know it's silly but it seemed that way we knew she was alright, even though we'd just talked ten to the dozen for however long.

"She's alright, love" Adam said. He had the phone gripped tight in his hand and his hand against his heart.

"I'm so glad, Adam. Really. I don't ever want to go through that again."

"We won't, love. We won't." I didn't think at the time how he could be so sure. I mean it was just words said to make me feel better because to be honest, I was still not back to earth, if you know what I mean? I was so tense and uptight and then, for the first time in hours, I remembered the baby. "I'd better lie down, Adam. I have to rest, remember what the doctor said?"

"Yes, quick, lie down and I'll make you a cuppa. Get some fluids back into you." Adam started to fuss over me, then went into the kitchen and put the kettle on. I have to say that cup of tea was one of the best I'd ever had.

"I'd forgotten about the baby in all the…"

"Excitement? Yeah, me too. I was just so worried…"

"About Sarah. I know. I can't believe it now, it seems like it was a bad dream."

"Bloody nightmare!"

We both laughed, but it was a laugh that was more of relief than humour. It had been a very tense time, what, five or six hours, tops? You never know how much worrying you can get done in so short a time but we must have set some new world records.

"Do you think we should fly back?" I asked Adam. I had to confess that now I knew she was fine and would be home soon I didn't want to cut our vacation short. I really wanted to stay here, at least until we knew if the IVF had taken. If it didn't then we had to go back for a second go and that would be so much easier, not to mention cheaper, from Manchester.

"No, no need, love. Sarah assured us she is perfectly fine and they only kept her in for observation just to be on the safe side, and I'm glad they did but there's no need to rush back to Brissie. Besides, that would be the worst thing for you and the baby."

"Providing it all worked, of course."

"It worked, love. Trust me. It worked."

There was, of course, no rational reason why Adam would know that for certain, not as certain as he seemed, but then love isn't rational either, is it?

And The Winner Is...

The clinic had told me that it would be two weeks, fourteen days, a fortnight (yes, they said it just like that!) before I would know for sure if I were pregnant or not. They made a big deal about how there was no point testing for it earlier because the chance of a false positive was very high with IVF and if it turned out to be a false positive we would be more upset than if we waited and got a true negative. So bang on Day 14 I tested again to see if the positive we'd got on Day 10 was a false positive or the real thing.

I know, I should have waited and if it had turned out to be a false positive we would have been upset but the fact was, neither of us could wait another day! I don't know who was worse, Adam or myself but we were both jumping with joy the first time and even more exuberant the second time. When I say jumping, I mean Adam was actually jumping up and down he was so happy. I wanted to but realised that wouldn't be good for the baby so I sat down and just kicked my legs around a bit, punched the air and smiled so wide the top of my head nearly came off. We were ecstatic!

So why at my age, and I was closer to 50 than 40, did we want a baby all over again? If I had a dollar for every time I have been asked that question I could have paid for the IVF twice over. If they made it a quid for every question it would cover our airfares, too! I remember Adam being asked this by some family friend or whoever, I forget exactly now but it was someone in the UK. We'd just got the great news (for the second time) and decided we'd celebrate. I remember the first time I was pregnant I'd had a shandy, I think it had been. This time there was no way I was taking even the slightest risk and I made sure the only person tasting anything remotely alcoholic was Adam.

We went to the club to play a few games of bingo and have a drink. It was the only thing open that night being a Monday, and Mondays around the world hardly being the most lively of nights. When I say 'club', it's not like the big registered clubs near our place, just across the border in Tweed Heads or what have you. No row upon row of poker machines, lots of bars and restaurants and headlining shows. Our local club in the UK was a converted semi-detached house at the end of the street. The street was like something out of Coronation Street, all pre-war terraced council houses with a narrow pavement leading to a cobbled, narrow street, now virtually a one way affair because of the cars parked on both sides.

The club was warm, friendly and a what you see is what you get sort of a place. The cash house prize was only a few quid but it was only 50p per card and the drinks were cheap, too. We were taking a break from the bingo, Adam was up the bar getting a round in and I noticed one of the other patrons chatting to him. He was the husband of the lady at the back of my mum's, a long distance lorry driver, forever away in Europe or sat there at the bar and boasting about smuggling fags back duty-free from Belgium. I saw Adam laugh, then try to move away, drinks on a tray poised between himself and the neighbour, like a barrier of some kind. Then the man leaned in and said something in Adam's ear and laughed as he leaned back. Adam didn't find it that funny and just turned on his heel and headed over to our table. I watched as the man just kind of shrugged and turned back to the bar.

"What was all that about, Adam?" I asked when he arrived at our table and began spreading the drinks around. We were sharing the table with my mum and dad and the neighbour from next door but two, Kerry. Kerry was my age and had lived in her house all her life, much as my parents had lived in theirs. Kerry was my age and had inherited the place from her parents. She'd never married and I figured she probably never would, given I was certain she batted for the other side, if you know what I mean. Not that there's anything wrong with that, these days. Just I'd always suspected she preferred the girls to the fellas. It was just a pity she was on her own these days. Had the house to herself and just too old fashioned I suppose to 'come out', as they say.

"Nothing, pet. Just some stupid drunken bollocks. You know what Vera's husband is like when he's at home."

"Actually I don't, love. Only met him the once, if you recall."

"Well, take no notice, he just has a funny way about him." Which was Adam's way of saying he was not worth worrying about, or getting to know. I have to admit, though, I was curious and so I pressed the point.

"Whatever he said, he seemed to think it was funny and you didn't." I left it there in the hope Adam would pick it up and continue the conversation, but not my Adam. Too clever to get caught out if he doesn't want to be, him.

"Yes, you're right" was all he said and he took a big sip of his pint.

"So, what did he say?"

"Who? What did who say?"

"Vera's bloody husband! The bloke you were speaking too just a moment ago at the bar." Adam could be obtuse when he chose to be and it seemed he chose to be here and now.

"Oh, Vera's husband. Freddie. Well, that's not his real name, is it?"

"How would I know, Adam, I've never met him except that once when mum and I were chatting with Vera over the back fence and he came out of the coal shed, other than that, I don't even know his name. Is it really Freddie?"

"No, 'course not. His surname is Merkree, or McMerkree or some'at, hence Freddie."

"I don't get it?" I confess it was all beyond me. I had no idea what Vera's last name was, she wasn't a local and neither was Freddie. Both of them had moved in off the Claremont Estate when that got pulled down what, ten years ago? So they weren't 'locals' in the true meaning of the word. You needed a direct line back before the war to be a local on our estate. "Why call him 'Freddie' when his name is…" and then I got it. "Oh, yeah, I get it!"

"Freddie Mercury, the lead singer of Queen!" Adam and I said it at the same time and Kerry joined in while mum and dad just laughed.

We all began to natter at once so Adam's redirection trick worked as I quite forgot to press him for whatever it was Freddie had said to him. We were at home, sitting on the sofa watching the late night talk show band play a musical number when I remembered and asked Adam again.

"So what did Freddie say to you, love? Back at the club." I noticed he went silent, then half turned away and he mumbled something about it not mattering. I pressed the point, though. My women's intuition telling me there was something amiss here.

"It was nothing, you know, the usual banter about being parents again at our age, all that sort of thing."

I gave Adam another look and then went back to watching the television. That wasn't it. There was something else, something he wasn't telling me but probing directly wasn't going to prise it out of him. Whatever had been said, Adam had not taken it as a joke or anything remotely amusing. I know the look that went across his face at that time and that Freddie was a half sentence away from getting thumped. I also knew the look Adam had on that moment and that was his don't push it look. Alright Adam Clarkson. I can wait. I won't forget but I will be waiting and watching and sooner or later you will tell me, one way or another. He always does. There are no secrets between us, at least not for long of forever.

I filed all of these details away for future 'mulling' over. It might make better sense in the future, when other things have revealed themselves. I just went back to enjoying the evening as it wound to a close and I let my mind wander around freely, solving little dilemmas like where would the baby sleep, what would it wear, what would we call him or her and so on.

The main thing was I was pregnant. Again. I could barely contain my excitement, it was just like the first one all over again, and the second one. The same, but different, just like both of the first two pregnancies had been different in their own way. Same morning sickness but different intensity, far worse with Ethan than Sarah. I had cravings both times, just very different. With Ethan it was garlic. Everything had to have garlic in it and I even tried garlic powder on my fruit salad. Sarah was like I'd become a vampire, or is it werewolves that can't stand garlic? Anyway, with her it was condensed milk. I think I consumed the entire Carnation factory production for the twelve weeks of my second trimester. I had it on lasagna, ice cream, rice pudding, even fried rice. I wonder what the craving will be this time, I remember thinking just before I nodded off.

Age Is Just A Number

"Are you going to tell me, Adam Clarkson, or not?" I had had enough of Adam moping around since we came back from the club the other night and I knew the best way to resolve the problem was to have it out with him. Not in public, that's not our way. We've had a few 'differences of opinion' over the many years we've been married but we keep them few and far between, behind closed doors and we always make sure we thrash it out, verbally, then kiss and make up. Adam and I are in it for the long haul and we know if something is broken, then you don't chuck it out, you fix it.

"Tell you what, exactly?"

"What it is the heck that's got you dragging your chin round the place like someone stole your dog, treated it better than you did and now it doesn't want to come home."

"You what? I mean, I beg your pardon? Stole my dog and…"

"You know what I mean, Adam. C'mon love, this is me you're trying to fool. I know something is bothering you and I know it was that Freddie Mercury bloke at the club last Monday. C'mon! Cough!"

Adam knew I wasn't going to be fobbed off and I could see by the change in his expression I had hit the nail on the head. It was that Freddie character who did this to Adam; set him off somehow. Adam walked into the kitchen and took a seat at the big table there, pulling one back for me to sit next to him on. I flicked the switch on the jug and set up the cups with coffee, sugar and milk, then made the two cuppas as the water had boiled just on cue. We both took a tentative sip and put the cup back, almost like we were some kind of street mime act. I took Adam's hands in mine, looked him in the eyes and took a deep breath.

"I'm going to be bloody retired by the time the baby leaves school, love."

"What? What do you mean… is this what that Freddie…" I was confused to say the least. I thought Freddie had said something earth shattering to Adam, you know, like telling him a long kept family secret like him and I were actually related or something really devastating like that. I'd just been reading in the women's magazine my mum took in about a brother and sister, separated at birth, meeting each other 30 years later, falling in love, having a kid and only then discovering they were siblings. You can imagine how life changing that kind of news would be.

This was the kind of thing I was expecting from Adam, given how he had been moping for days now.

"I will be over 65 by the time the baby turns 18."

"Is that all, love?" I really didn't understand how this was so devastating to Adam.

"Is that all? I'll be a senior citizen. A pensioner. Elderly. Aged. Old!"

"Well so will I, I mean so will I be 65. We're the same age remember? In fact, you're only two months and five days older than I am." We used to joke about this, years ago. How we would both be on the pension and bent over a walking frame together, living out our twilight years in a home by the sea, like Darby and Joan, the archetypal English old couple.

"Yes, but it's different…"

"Different? Because I'm a woman?"

"Well, yes. I mean, no. You know what I mean!" And we both laughed again.

"Didn't you think about this before you suggested we have another baby. You usually think through all the angles before you do something."

"I did, I do, well, not this. I mean I didn't really give it much thought until that Freddie bloke mentioned it."

"What did he say that has had such a huge effect on you?" I confess I was curious because what ever he had said it had really hit the mark with Adam.

"He said I shouldn't drink too much as I didn't want to be buried by the baby before it was old enough to have a drink with me on its 18th birthday."

I looked at Adam and I could see that had hit home. A throw away remark in a pub, meant to be light hearted banter, it had really made a mark. "Adam, that's it? That's all he said?" I really didn't think it was that big a deal, even though Adam obviously felt otherwise.

"Love, it made me think. I mean, really. I will be retiring the same year the kid leaves school and goes off to university or whatever he or she decides to do. What if I don't make it that far? What if something happens to me at work or I have an accident like Sarah, only serious."

"What if your mother was your father, you wouldn't be here, would you?"

"I know, I know. It's just, well…"

"It's just we get a glimpse of our own mortality when we see our kids."

"That's pretty deep for…"

"For a woman? For me?" I teased him a little.

"You know what I mean, love. It's pretty deep, but spot on. Yeah. We do get a glimpse at our own mortality when we look at our kids. We look back at our parents and we know they won't be around forever. I mean we've both been lucky with ours, in their seventies and still fit and healthy.

It must be even more... I dunno. More real, more unavoidable when you're their age but, well, having a kid now and knowing we'll be close to their age by the time he or she is an adult..."

"That's life, pet. That's how it is, how it's meant to be. I mean look at Carol. King, not Witherton. Carol King, remember her? She was pregnant with her first the same time I was having Sarah and her husband walked into a steel beam at work, remember?"

"Carol King? Oh yeah. Ronnie King was her husband. Actually the steel beam fell on him, the shackle opened. I remember because..."

"Yeah, well she was left a widow at what, 23, 24? A kid on the way and no father. She nearly lost the baby but she didn't. She got on with it, right? A few years later she met that bloke and they migrated to Canada."

"New Zealand. They went to Auckland, I remember she wrote to your mum and said the day they got there the place was closed, boring as hell, she said."

"Yeah, that's right. Auckland. Anyway, she loves it there now, three more kids last I heard."

"Jeez, how long ago was that?"

"Last Easter. She's a Facebook friend. I told you I'd caught up with most of my old class, remember?"

"Yeah, I'll get around to that one of these days. Amazing thing, Face..."

"Anyway, my point is this, Adam Clarkson. Life goes on. It deals you a bad hand now and then but if it is your time to go then stiff cheddar. Off you trot. Until then you keep waking up and having the best day you can. Right?"

"Right love."

"And don't go worrying about how old anyone will be in ten or twenty years time. We'll all be ten or twenty years older, nothing we can do about it. Might as well get on with life, right?"

"Right love but then that's the point, isn't it?"

"Huh?"

"You get on with life but that means you have to care for the life you create. I mean, I was brought up to believe that if you are going to make kids then you have to bring them up. You don't walk out on your missus and find someone else just because it gets too hard. You get up and you get stuck in. You do your best for your family, you put..."

"You put them before yourself. I know, Adam. We were both brought up like that and we both do that, don't we? So what's your problem?"

"Well, a kid needs a dad who can play with him. Or her. You know, not some doddering old codger who can't..."

"I don't believe you, Adam. When will you ever be a doddering old codger? Look at my dad. Would you call him a doddering old codger?"

"No. He'd probably bloody thump me!" Which had us laughing again. Adam was a good man, my dad had said that when I married him. He stood next to me at the top of the aisle as the organ played the Wedding March and all heads had turned to watch him walk me down the aisle. 'He's a good man, your Adam, pet. Look after him, alright?' Those were his exact words and I can still hear them to this day. He did his best for us, never one to drink his wages up against a wall, always there for us.

"You'll be fine, love. In fact, you'll be a better dad for this one because you know what to expect. You know what to do. We didn't have a clue with Ethan and not much more of an idea when Sarah came along but we managed, didn't we?" He nodded and gave me a kiss on the cheek.

"Thanks pet. I love you."

"I love you too, Adam."

The Baby Boom

"OK, love. Yes, that's terrific news. I dunno, we'll probably come home now. Maybe we'll have them together, side by side!" I hung up the phone and just sat there. To be honest, as pleased as I had made out to be on the phone to Sarah, I was really feeling very much the opposite. Sarah had called and told me she was pregnant. Her and Stewart were going to have a baby and it seemed the due date was within a day or two of mine.

I had three hours to myself until Adam came back from golf. Three hours when I knew his mobile would be switched off, if he'd bothered to take it with him. Golf time was 'my time', he was fond of reminding me. I never bothered telling him there was precious little 'my time' for me. I didn't have much to do, just make this baby but hanging about the house isn't the same when you're pregnant as it is when you're not. When you aren't expecting you can do anything you want to. You usually don't do anything other than what you normally do, which for most of us probably isn't that much but it's the fact you can if you want to whereas when you are pregnant you can't. You have to always think of the baby before yourself.

I didn't mind, really and I certainly didn't begrudge the baby for anything. Afterall, he, or she, didn't ask to be made. Nine months, well 266 days or 8 days shy of nine months, is a long time to wait for the 'blessed event' but I was grateful I wasn't a horse. They had 340 days to wait. For elephants it's even longer, 640 days. Twenty two months. Kangaroos only had to wait 45 days but then they had it in the pouch for months and months; but at least it was out and they could hop around a bit. I mentally gave myself a shake and told me to stop talking so wet. I had been surfing the web and come across a page on Wikipedia that listed mammalian gestation periods, fascinating stuff but not something I'd mention to Adam. He'd never let me live it down!

"I'm home love!" echoed down the hallway, followed by the sound of a golf buggy banging into the wall and then the door to the storage area under the stairs being opened and the buggy wrestling its way into where it hides out between games.

"I'm in here, in the conservatory." Which was a bit moot given he always finds me in the conservatory this time of the day. It is, I confess, my favourite room in the house. The view over the typical English garden can hold my interest for hours, no matter which season it is. I love the autumn the best because the leaves that cover the ground add such lovely russet tones. Winter is nice if it is snowing but otherwise it's too stark, too grey and black and bare. Spring and Summer are lovely, but then they're supposed to be, aren't they?

"Got a new handicap! I'm now at…"

"Sarah's pregnant." I know it was a bit brutal but honestly, I don't really follow all that handicap nonsense anyway and I figured my news trumped his any day of the week.

"You what? What did you say? Sarah?"

"Yes, love. Sarah. Your daughter. Our daughter. She's pregnant."

"With a baby?"

"Of course with a baby you gormless bugger! What'd you think, a koala bear?" We both laughed and Adam gave me a huge hug.

"That's fantastic news! Her and Stewart, right?"

"Well I certainly hope so!"

"When's she due?"

"About the same time as me, give or take a day or two."

"Same day? That's fantastic! Who'd have thought it?"

"I know. I wouldn't."

"You don't sound as happy as I would have expected you to, Sue. What's the matter?"

"Nothing. Well, it's just…"

"Just what? Not jealous are you? She's stealing our thunder or something?"

"Don't be daft. No, its not that at all. I mean, I'm thrilled. We're going to be grandparents. Our baby will be the uncle or aunty and they will be the same age."

"That'll be a laugh, especially if Sarah goes first. Then the niece or nephew will be older than their aunty or uncle."

"Yes, a real hoot, as they say."

Adam could tell I wasn't completely comfortable with this news and to be honest, I didn't know why I felt this way, I just did. He sat down at the table a few minutes later after making us both a cuppa and looked me straight in the eye in that way he has when he's worried about me.

"C'mon, pet. What's bothering you? About Sarah having the baby, I mean."

"I know what you mean, I just don't know why I'm feeling this… this… this, I don't know what this is. I'm just not a hundred percent with it, that's all."

"Sarah will make a great mum. Afterall, she had the best teacher."

"Thanks, love but it's not that. I dunno. It's not Sarah I'm worried about, come to think of it."

"Stewart?"

"Yeah. Stewart."

Adam took a sip of his coffee and looked out the conservatory windows into the garden. He took another sip then put his cup down and took my hands in his across the table.

"I know what you mean. I mean, on thinking about it, I guess we really don't know Stewart that well, do we? They've been together what, two, three years more or less but still, what do we know about him?"

"We've never even met his parents. I know Marg has talked about Nathan plenty of times but he never comes around when we have a BBQ, Marg always comes alone if she turns up."

"She's only been the once, actually, love."

I thought about that and Adam was right. She had only been the once and that was years ago, back when she first started working for us and we had the company Christmas party at our place. The company was too big now to have hundreds of people tramping the flower beds and tossing empties into the pool so we always have it somewhere else, catered for and all. She never brought Nathan to any of those parties, either.

"Well we know Stewart, well enough, though. He's alright, isn't he?"

"Yes, I suppose. He seems a nice enough bloke but…"

"But what, Sue?"

I hesitated to say what was on my mind. Not because I couldn't say it to Adam. I can tell Adam anything and I say to him whatever I am thinking because I trust him. He's never once put me down for having an opinion different to his. He might not agree with me all the time, or even do what I want him to but he does listen and he does take notice and you can't ask fairer than that from men, can you?

"I just have this niggly little feeling, you know? Just something I can't quite put a finger on, do you know what I mean?"

Adam took another sip of his coffee and gave that some thought. He took two more sips before he put the cup down, stood up and went to gaze out the window at the garden.

"You're right, love. As usual. I don't… I mean there's something I don't quite get about him, you know? I've always felt this but I brushed it aside because Sarah was always talking him up and Marg speaks so well of him and all. I dunno. I thought it was because I'm her dad and you know what they say; how no bloke is good enough for your own daughter, even though you're good enough for someone else's. I thought I was just being paranoid, or over protective; jealous maybe."

"Well, there's not much we can do about it, is there?"

"You're right. Again, love. Not much we can do, really. Too late now, she's in the club!"

"You never know, it might do her the world of good, having a wee one to look after. Might settle young Stewart down a bit, too."

"Settled me down."

"Yeah, but you weren't Stewart. You were different, Adam. And you wanted to have a family. And we were married already."

"That's not important these days, Sue. Not anymore. No stigma attached like there was when we were born or even when Ethan and Sarah were born. Times have changed a lot and mostly for the good."

Adam was right. These days people had the kids first and then had them at the wedding as page boys and flower girls. I guess it doesn't matter nowadays whether the parents are legally married or not, so long as they love each other. A bit like the change in thinking about same sex marriages. I used to be dead against same sex marriages at one time but now I think so long as they love each other, what business is it of mine or Adam's? We used to think it wasn't fair on the kids if they were then allowed to adopt but the two best renters of our holiday flats were a couple of blokes who had been together for nearly twenty years. Both of them had kids from normal marriages before they came out or whatever they call it. They used to rent both apartments and put their kids in one and stay in the other. Now their kids are all grown up and the older ones have families of their own. So who's to judge? Surely what is important is how they treat each other and look after each other. I just hoped Stewart was the type to stick around and I said as much to Adam.

"That is the sixty four thousand dollar question, Sue. When the baby arrives and the reality sinks in; will he stick it out?"

"His dad didn't."

"What do mean? How do you know that?"

"Marg told me. She said once that Nathan had walked out when Stewart was three or something. She blamed his wife, Stewart' mother. Said she was too hard to live with."

"So did he see his son on weekends, then?"

"Apparently he had nothing to do with them until Stewart turned sixteen. That's when he met Marg and she basically talked him into getting back in touch with his son. Nearly got him thrown in jail, though."

"Why's that?"

"Child support. Hadn't paid a cracker for twelve years and social services still had him on file."

"So what happened?"

"Marg didn't go into much detail. I think from what she said, Stewart' mum basically agreed to waive any outstanding child support payments if Nathan would be the dad Stewart should have had."

"She must have torn up, what, thousands?"

"I'd imagine so. A dozen years of even a hundred a week is a lot of money to wave goodbye but I guess after getting by without his help for that long she figured it was more important Stewart had a relationship with his biological father."

"A deadbeat dad, in other words? I really can't stand blokes like that. I mean, have your fun but then stand up to your responsibilities, you know?"

"Yes, well, there are far too many Nathans in this world, Adam. I just hope his son doesn't carry his dad's genes as far as that's concerned. Hopefully he knows how important a father is to a child and he does his best to be a good one."

"Not like that rat father of his."

"That rat father of his is cleaning our holiday flats, remember?"

"Oh, yeah. I'd forgotten about that for a moment. Bugger. If I had known I wouldn't have agreed to let him and Marg handle things while we are away."

"So who would you have gotten to do it?"

"There are dozens of strata management mobs that could have done it, Sue. I could have asked any real estate agent to organise it, I was just too bloody cheap. I hate paying them for doing nothing more than having a list of people keen to do the work and sending them to us."

"That's not like you, Adam. You usually appreciate people who have the connections and the know-how. I know you make a few quid putting people together for various things."

"Fair enough. Anyway, what are we doing, love?"

"What do you mean?"

"Are we staying or going back?"

"Going back?"

"Yeah, to have the baby in Oz and to be with Sarah while she has hers. I mean she uses our GP, you have the same Gyno, you could do all your pre-natals together, make it easy to arrange the transport and all." Adam was always quick to figure out the details, make a plan, organise things. He had already put the Stewart as a good father issue to one side. He wouldn't forget it nor would he simply let it go, but he does have the knack of being able to compartmentalize things. Right now he had put Stewart and his fathering style away in one compartment while he opened another and started figuring out the logistics of having two babies delivered to the family around the same time. Maybe even at the same time.

"Not sure, yet, Adam. I need to give it some more thought." To be honest I had made up my mind while I waited for Adam to come back from golf. Of course we would go back. Soon as we could. I wanted to be there for my baby girl's first baby and I wanted to make sure if her Stewart was wanting in any areas, she'd have me and her dad to fall back on. That's the kind of family we are but I was under no illusions every family saw it like we did. I'm not saying we're perfect or the best way to be, not at all. All I am saying is this is how we are and this is the way we think it should be and how you live your life is up to you. But if you become a part of this family, then we expect you to do as we would and that means being there for each other.

***

We spent the next few weeks finishing off the things we had planned to spread out over the next five months or so. We went to York and walked down the Shambles, then off to Durham and the old cathedral and came back through the Lake District with a side trip to Wales. It was lovely, just the two of us, well three if you count the baby, enjoying the freedom to go where we wanted to and spend as long as we liked, wherever we chose to go. We even had a weekend trip planned to see Paris but we cut that short when the telephone call came. It was after three in the morning and at first I didn't understand what Adam was saying, I was still half asleep as he handed me the phone.

"Love, it's Sarah. She's in tears."

"Sarah? What's the matter love?" Sarah started crying and talking all at the same time and I couldn't understand a word. "Calm down, I can't understand what you're…"

"What is it, love?" Adam had his head next to the phone trying to hear so I hit the speaker button.

"… and I don't know what to do." I'd missed the first bit when I had to take the phone away from my ear to find the speaker button.

"Say it again, love. Slowly."

"Mum, he hit me!"

Part Three - Sarah

It's All My Fault

I felt something for Stewart the first time I saw him. He has something about him I can't put my finger on but you know it when you see it; you know what I mean? To me he is a good looking bloke, well built and really funny. He always treated me like I was his princess, at least at first. It was only later, when I stuffed everything up for him that he started to change. It was all my fault. I know that and so does he. And his mum, and dad, and Marg. Everyone but my own parents could see I was the one causing all the trouble and making him angry.

I don't do it on purpose, in fact I usually have no idea I'm doing it. It really all kicked off after the car accident. Stewart was driving and we got hit up the rear end by some idiot who wasn't paying attention. Stewart had just swung into the lane and had to stop because the traffic light went red and there was a camera at that intersection. So what else was he expected to do? I remember the bang and the jolt and it sounded like a ten ton truck had fallen on the boot, it was so loud.

"You alright, Sarah?"

"Yeah. No. I dunno. Oh, my neck!" I had whiplash, I was sure of it. We had been hit so hard I was thrown forwards against the dash, then flung back into the seat so hard I'm sure I heard a crack, even above all the noise of the car behind us parking itself in the boot.

"Bloody idiot!" This was the driver of the car behind us. He'd gotten out and come up to Stewart' window, shaking his fist and looking like he was going to explode. "You cut me off!"

"Piss off, mate! You hit me up the arse, you're at fault!" Stewart was getting out of the car, the man taking a step back and still going on.

"You cut me off! Right on the orange!"

"You hit me. You're in the wrong. I had to stop. The light went red, didn't it?" Stewart was telling the truth. The light had gone red just as we were about to go through on the orange. I'd barely enough time to yell out 'camera!' and Stewart hit the anchors. If he'd gone through the red he'd be up for a fine and loss of points and he only had one or two left as it was. No way were we going to get in trouble because the wanker behind us was travelling too close and too fast. Like Stewart said, he hit us.

"Well you hit us and my girlfriend's got whiplash now. We'll probably need an ambulance and your insurance company isn't going to like you mate!" Stewart was almost laughing as he said it. He had looked like he was going to deck the bloke at first, but he got his temper under control and that's another thing I love about him. It seems I'm the only thing that sets him off. It's because I'm special, he tells me. Special in his heart.

They went at it back and forth until finally the man realised he was in the wrong and pretty much admitted his guilt, although not in so many words as Stewart explained to me later. The back of my car was pushed right in, there was no longer a boot, just crumpled metal and broken tail lights. The front of his car was shorter, too. His radiator had shit itself and there was greenish water everywhere. The front bumper panel thing was on the road and his headlights were all cracked and splintered. I didn't think he'd be driving it away and I was not so sure we would either.

"I'm not admitting fault or liability. Let's exchange particulars and we'll leave it to our insurance companies to fight over it. Do you have your Driver's License? Here's mine." He handed over his license and Stewart told me to get a pen and some paper from the car.

I was a bit slow on the uptake and he snapped, "hurry friggin' up!" I fumbled around in the glove box and found a pen and then an old envelope on the floor in the back and handed them to Stewart. The man was just finishing writing down Stewart' particulars. He handed back his license then went to the front of the car to get the rego number of my car.

"We'll have to call the police and wait for them. My car needs towing and you said your girlfriend is injured."

"What? nah, there's no need to call the cops. You hit me up the bum, that's clear enough for the insurance companies, right?" Stewart seemed rather tense, as if he was keen to leave. I wasn't sure if the insurance company would want us to stay for the police, afterall, we were in the right, he hit us up the bum. Stupid me made things worse by trying to persuade him maybe the old guy was right and we were better off calling the cops.

"Maybe we should, Stewart. I mean he's in the wrong and my neck is killing me…"

"Shut the fuck up, alright?" Stewart snapped back like one of those really bored, pissed off lions at the zoo. The ones all the kids and that tease until finally they snap and roar at you. I think that's probably a bit cruel but otherwise the bloody things just sit there all day and do nothing. Who wants to pay sixty, seventy bucks a ticket to get in and see a sleeping lion? Well Stewart was just like a lion that someone, me, had just woken up. He went off then. Calling me a few bad names and letting me know how stupid I was and I guess he was right. I should've kept my mouth shut and let him handle it.

"Sorry, doll" I tried to calm him down but he was off and going. Maybe he'd hit his head on the steering wheel? I felt like everything was all my fault and really, I guess it was. I had suggested we take my car because he had made a big fuss last night when he went to pick up the pizza how he'd have no petrol to get to work and even though he hates driving my 'Jap rice burner', he has to drive. He says a woman can't drive as good as a man can. At first he said he drove everywhere because I was his princess and therefore I deserved a chauffeur, that I was too beautiful to hide behind the steering wheel. That was at first; a long time ago now it seems.

"Don't fucking 'sorry doll' me. It's your fault we are in this mess. If you hadn't insisted we got pizza last night…"

"But you suggested we…"

"Anything's better than the crap you cooked for tea the night before."

"I told you the first time we went out I can't cook. I don't even like eating, much." Which is true. I am so skinny people think I am anorexic but I'm not. I just don't eat much, I guess. I have never made myself throw up after eating, although I think that's Bulimia but I'm not sure. Anyway, I know what my mum says but I do not have an eating disorder. I just don't like to be fat.

"That's fine for you but some of us need to…"

"Are you two going to have a domestic all day or should we get on with this. I'm calling the police." The man seemed pretty angry himself now. He pulled out an iPhone and started to dial. Stewart snatched the phone from him and then gave it back, almost in the same motion.

"Look, I told you. Don't bother. You want to call a tow truck, up to you but I gotta get my girlfriend to the hospital to have her neck checked." He turned away and went to the car, got in and then poked his head out of the window and said; "Get in!" I got in. The man came to his window and put his hand on the door where the glass slides into it.

"Mate, you piss off and that's leaving the scene of an accident. You'll get in real trouble for that."

"Get your hands off my car!" Stewart glared at the man. I couldn't see his face I know but I could see the way his shoulders were tensed and I knew he'd have his glare on his face. I'd seen him glare at some lads that had tried to pick me up at the club one night. I thought there was going to be a fight but the other blokes just laughed it off and ignored him. I pleaded with Stewart not to start a fight, I mean there was three or four of them and he said he wouldn't fight them but next time I should be more careful and not slut around. I mean I wasn't!

"You drive off before the police come and that's an offence. That's all I'm saying." The man had backed away a step or two from the car and let go of the door. He stood there as Stewart started the car, checked over his shoulder, then drove off. He stuck his fist out of the window and gave the man the finger, then turned the corner and headed for the hospital.

"I hope you don't get in trouble, Stewart." I tried to sound sweet and concerned, because I was, but he took it the wrong way.

"Screw him and screw you. You caused this. You made us have pizza. You made me use up my petrol. You have a crappy car and you…" He continued like this all the way to the hospital. I just sat there, said nothing and cried as quietly as I could. I didn't look at him, I looked out the window. My neck hurt and I knew he was right. It was all my fault. I swore to myself I'd make it up to him.

While we waited in Emergency I called Marg at the office and told her what had happened. She was stunned and asked if we had admitted fault. Apparently even if you are in the wrong you never say sorry or that it was your fault or the insurance doesn't pay or something. I told her the other bloke hit us in the rear and she said we were alright then. She asked if the police had come but I said I didn't know, we'd driven off before they could have arrived. That made her go quiet.

She said if they turn up at the hospital or come to see us at home or work, say nothing until she had a chance to talk to us about what to say. She asked me to put Stewart on and I did. They were talking for a while, Stewart moved away from me after he said 'hello' and 'yeah, right next to me'. I asked him what she had said to him and he told me if anyone asks who was driving, say it was me.

"Me? Do you mean say it was you, Stewart, or me, me?" I was confused to say the least. I thought he would blow his stack again but he didn't. I guess he had calmed down after the adrenalin faded away or whatever happens in these crisis situations.

"You, lover." I felt all warm when he called me 'lover'. He has this way of saying it, you know he means it and you are the only person in his world.

"OK, but, well, why?"

"Because it is your car and the insurance doesn't cover me."

"Yes it does. I'm sure of it. In fact I know it does. Dad put the car in his name and paid the extra for drivers under 25. That includes you, not just me."

"You think that's the case but Marg was telling me it is only you that's covered."

"But my dad said…"

"Doesn't matter what Adam said, Marg does all the insurances for all the factory vehicles, remember? She pays the premiums, does the paperwork. She assures me your dad only paid for a nominated under 25 driver. That's you. Not me. Put me down as the driver and you don't get a cent!"

"But the other driver is in the wrong, remember? You said so. So did Marg. He hit us in the back."

"Yes, but his insurance company will try anything to get out of paying, won't they? I mean, they are the ones that pay for the repairs but you usually claim against your own policy first, then the insurance company claims against his insurance company and they fight it out amongst themselves."

"I didn't know that, lover." I like to call him lover too, especially when I'm trying to get back in his good books after doing stupid things. "I mean, that's why I need you, you know? I'd be lost without you, Stewart."

"Well then, sweetie cakes," another pet name I love to hear, even if it is pretty silly, "you do as I say. Tell them you were driving."

"But you gave the man your driver's license, not mine. He'll tell them it was you driving, not me."

"Marg said not to worry about that. I did mention it to her but she has this all figured out. We don't deny I gave him my license for him to copy the details from, because that would be stupid, right?" I nodded, not really sure why it was stupid but pretty sure that it was. "So when they ask why, I tell them he was acting all creepy and touchy feely with you, asking if you were hurt and feeling you up and so I gave my details so he wouldn't have your address. In case he was a pervert or a stalker!"

"But he never touched me. He just asked me if I were alright, remember?"

"Gawd, Sarah, sometimes you can be so dense. I know he didn't really touch you up. We just say that to explain why we didn't give him your driver's license when it was you who was driving. Understand?"

"Ahh! Yeah, I get it now. Brilliant, you are so smart Stewart." I knew it had been Marg who came up with this plan but it didn't hurt to give Stewart some praise.

"Sweet, lover. So you know what to say then?"

"Yes. I was driving but I didn't want to give him my driver's license because he had been feeling me up and I was worried he was a stalker."

"You got it, lover. Awesome." He smiled at me and I nearly fell off the chair. I hugged him instead and gave him a pash. Talk about bad timing, after waiting there for more than an hour, just as I was getting my Stewart back to loving me mode, they called our names and we went through the big plastic doors to be seen by the doctor.

Of Course You're The Father

"Sarah, we are going to keep you in overnight, OK?" I wasn't too happy about that, to be honest. I just wanted to go home. Me and Stewart could go back to our flat and take it easy, maybe take the next day off work and just spend some time together. It would give me a chance to make it up to him for the accident.

"Do I have to? I mean, I feel fine, really. I feel OK, just a bit of a headache coming on but I think that's the waiting around and…"

"It is more likely shock setting in." Shock? What did she mean?

"Shock? How do you mean? I'm not shocked or anything, just my neck is a bit sore and I'm getting a headache. Really, I would prefer to go home."

"I understand, Sarah. Shock can happen hours after the event. Delayed shock is probably one of the most dangerous complications from an accident like yours. You get out, you walk around, everything seems fine. Then a few hours later, shock sets in and you collapse."

"But, why? I feel fine."

"I'm talking about an acute stress reaction, not circulatory shock, which is a different thing altogether, but still very serious. It happens after someone has been in a very terrifying situation, like an accident, often due to feelings of fear and helplessness. It can be worse for women in your condition."

"I don't… I mean I…" I was confused. I admit I was frightened when the accident happened but we were just sitting there and then we were hit and then it was all over. I didn't have time to be frightened. Not then. I did start to feel a little upset and worried but that was just because she was talking about it. If she hadn't said anything I wouldn't be thinking about it.

"I really think it is best for both of you to stay overnight. It won't cost anything and surely, it's better to be safe than sorry, right Sarah?"

"Yes, um… both of us? You mean Stewart is staying overnight, too? Can we be in the same ward?" Spending the night in hospital next to Stewart wasn't as nice as spending it in the same bed but if I had to spend the night in hospital it was better than nothing.

"No, Stewart is fine. He will be sent home. He's just waiting for you, probably just needs to say goodbye till tomorrow and find out if you need anything. Besides, we don't have mixed wards in Pre-Natal."

"Pre-Natal? Isn't that where pregnant women…"

"Yes. I think it is better than in a general ward and beds there are few and far between, but we do have space in Pre-Natal and you qualify, so that's where we'll put you. Just to be sure, run a few more tests this afternoon and tomorrow morning and you should be fine, right to go."

This wasn't really registering, to be honest. "But what do you mean, 'my condition'? Or 'I qualify' for Pre-Natal? I'm not…"

"You're pregnant! Oh, dear, I'm sorry. I'm so sorry Sarah. I thought you knew. Yes, you're pregnant."

I was stunned, or gobsmacked as my dad would say. She started to tell me details like how pregnant I was and when it was due and what I needed to do now. There was so much information coming at me my head just swam and I really didn't take it all in.

"Here, this is a little information pack we put together, it tells you everything you need to know. Plus you can always visit the website, the address is there, on the back."

I was clutching the folder full of brochures and info sheets and basically just staring past the doctor at a plastic pop out poster showing someone's intestinal passages or whatever it was. One of those medical posters the drug companies hand out. I saw the reproductive organs on the female and how they were all squashed up when she was pregnant and it dawned on me that was what was going to happen to my insides in a few months. I mean, this was real and I was all alone in the room with a total stranger who had just told me the most important news of my life.

"I need to talk to Stewart" was all I could say.

"Is Stewart the father of the…"

"Of course he is!" I spat back, a little too harshly but I mean, who else could it be?

"I'm sorry, Sarah. I didn't mean to suggest…"

"No, sorry Doctor, my fault. I just, well, I didn't know, you know? I mean I'm stunned, I mean it's great news but we weren't planning on having a family or anything, well not officially and that but…"

"Well, you're having one now. Too early to tell if it will be a boy or a girl but not too early to start taking the best care of yourself and bubby."

"Bubby? Oh yes, the baby. I still can't believe it. I'm in sh…"

"Shock?" laughed the doctor. She smiled and said, "well if you have to be in some kind of shock, that is the best kind because it isn't the harmful kind!"

"I know, still, it is a shock, doc!" and we both laughed at my rhyme. When we stopped laughing I suddenly realised I had to tell Stewart and I felt a new emotion creeping in. I think it was fear. I really think I was scared to tell him and I couldn't figure out why. I told the doctor about this and we talked about what was the best thing to do. She advised me to say nothing today, just go to the ward, get tested and checked and make sure everything was alright and then tell him at a time and place of my choosing. She said that was what she would do but of course, I was free to run out and tell him right away; but we both knew I wouldn't do that. Maybe he was in shock too, or this might trigger some kind of, what did the doctor call it? Yeah, an acute stress reaction. No, best all round was to say nothing. I would enjoy my time in hospital thinking about how I was going to tell him we were going to be parents. I was sure he would be rapt. I knew he'd make a great dad, I just knew it.

***

"I am the father?" Stewart was mad. I hadn't seen him so worked up for a while, not since the accident. I had waited a couple of weeks, just didn't find the right time and place, you know? Now I had told him and he was not taking it as I had hoped. In fact, he wasn't taking it at all.

"Of course you are!" I was getting angry myself. How dare he? I mean, who else could be the father? "It's your baby, sweetie, there has never been anyone else. I love you." I knew I was close to tears but I forced myself not to break down and start blubbering. He hated it when I cried. Sometimes he hated that I was crying and tried to make me feel better, but lately he had just been angry that I was crying. Said it made my face ugly and he hated all the 'snot and tears'.

"Why the fuck did you go and get pregnant?"

"I didn't go and get pregnant! You made me pregnant! You! You know, you stuck your…"

"Don't be a smart arse, Sarah, you can't back it up."

"What do you mean by that?"

"Exactly! See, you're not even smart enough to know what I mean. I think you deliberately got pregnant to trap me into marrying you!"

I couldn't help it. I just burst into tears and I didn't give a stuff if he didn't like it or if my face was ugly. I felt ugly. I felt wretched, like I was nothing! I just turned away and faced the wall on my side of the bed and sobbed. No, it was more than just sobs, it was a full-on performance of misery. Absolute misery. I couldn't believe he was behaving like this. He was treating me like some kind of slut who got pregnant on purpose. Where was the love? Where was the 'you're the reason I stay alive, Sarah'? Just bullshit. Bullshit he spewed out to get me to do those things he liked. The stuff I hated to do but I did it for him because I loved him and I knew he wanted me to do it.

"Stop friggin crying, will ya? I have to think." He got up and sat on the edge of the bed, fumbling for his smokes. He lit up and I got a big whiff. I had given up smoking the moment the doctor told me I was pregnant. I didn't smoke much anyway. I only started because Stewart smoked.

66

Everyone in his family smoked. In between lighting up they'd moan on about the cost of cigarettes and the government screwing them with the taxes and how the tax from smokers paid for all the medical bills in the country. They never shut up about it.

"Stewart, please. The smoke isn't good for the baby. Even second-hand smoke, I mean…"

"What? Now you're telling me I can't fucking smoke in my own home? Well if it is so bad for the frigging baby, get out of the frigging room! Go on! Fuck off! Sleep on the fucking couch!"

"Stewart? I'm sorry, love…"

"Go on! Fuck off! Sleep on the couch."

"Stewart, please, let's talk about this…"

"Fuck you! I'll sleep on the fucking couch then!" He just grabbed his pillow and stormed out, slamming the door so hard I thought the ceiling would cave in on me. I was half sat up, leaning on one elbow and just lying there with my mouth wide open. I mean, I was in shock. Yeah, just like the doctor had said. I was feeling scared, helpless and to be honest, confused, terrified, everything all at once.

I wanted to rush out there, into the lounge and tell him I was sorry, I didn't mean to get pregnant. I thought for a second, just a second, I could get an abortion. I shuddered as the word formed in my head. I couldn't believe I thought that. But I did. I hadn't given that a single moment before now. It had never occurred to me to do anything other than have my baby and… well, have my baby and live happily ever after. I know, it's a fairy tale but that was how our romance had been. Right up until the car accident. Well, maybe a few months before that, but ever since I came out of the hospital it had been pretty much one screw up after another. It was as if I couldn't do anything properly, I just kept hurting him and doing silly things that made him angry. Like this.

I laid there for an hour, not sleeping, not being able to sleep. I just kept thinking how I could make it right with Stewart. I wanted this baby, his baby. I wanted his baby. I knew he would change his mind. He just needed time to let it sink in. It was my fault, again. Of course. It was the way I had told him. No wonder he thought it was all a trap. I mean, I had made him dinner, with candles and a rose. Then we had made love and I had done that thing for him, the one he likes more than any of the other things and then I figured it was alright to tell him. I was wrong. I know now. I ruined it for him, his special thing. I should have just waited another day, told him in the morning on the way to work. I was selfish. I just wanted to tell him, to get it said and then we could move on. I'd been sitting on this for weeks and I just had to tell him, tell someone. I hadn't told anyone, not even my best friends, just my mum and she told Dad and I only told her last night. I called her when Stewart was out with his mates for a few drinks at the pub. I didn't want to go, alcohol's no good for the baby and I knew if I went he'd want me to drink something. I could have gone with him last night, it wasn't his 'Boy's Night'. He has one of those one night every week, usually a Friday but sometimes Thursdays, never Saturdays because he says Saturday night is our night, the best night of the week. Or he used to say it. Hasn't said it for a while. Anyway, I didn't go. I rang me mum instead. Told her the good news. I didn't tell her I hadn't told Stewart though. I think she thought he already knew. I didn't want to have to go through a lengthy explanation, not at international call rates when it was my phone. I didn't want her ringing me back to continue the conversation either. It would only make her anxious; I know my mum. Better to tell her it was all sweet and leave it like that.

I went into the bathroom and cleaned up. My makeup was a mess from my crying. I put new makeup on because I was not going to sleep, not just then. I was going to make it up to Stewart. Get him off the couch and back to bed. I'd do whatever he wanted me to do. I just wanted him back and happy.

He was facing the back of the couch when I went into the living room. I knelt down beside him and started to stroke his hair. I kissed his neck and pressed myself against his back. He just lay there, ignoring me. I knew he wasn't asleep, I can tell. He was just lying there, stiff, angry, tense.

"I'm sorry love" I said. I meant it too.

"Piss off."

"Stewart, please!"

"Piss off and go back to your bed. I don't want to talk to you, I don't want to see your face, I don't really want you in my flat."

His flat? My dad owns this flat. He lets us live here for a tiny rent, puts it down as part of our salary package or something. It was more my flat than his. I almost told him this but I stopped myself, just in time. No point making him even angrier.

"I'm sorry Stewart. I want to make it up to you. I'll…" I left the rest unsaid but he knew what I meant because he could feel what I was doing. He pretended not to be interested but I knew better. It was working. He rolled over and looked at me. I looked up into his eyes, reflected like two dots of light in the grey darkness of the flat.

"Don't piss me off again, OK?" he shook me by the shoulders and I promised him I wouldn't, I promised him I'd be good. Then I made good on my promise.

Just Four Words

"So what about the money?"

"What money, lover?"

"The friggin' insurance money, for the car accident."

"But that was my car. I put the insurance money in my bank account, sweetie."

Stewart glowered at me, the colour rising visibly from his neck to his forehead. It was like one of those cartoons where the person goes redder and redder then steam comes out of their ears and you hear the whistle blow. Stewart was about to blow, I could see that. Hell, blind Freddy could see that. I couldn't take a step back, I was already against the wall near the front door to our apartment. I had just walked in, closed the door behind me and turned around and there was Stewart, looming over me, angry and red and ready to explode.

"It was my friggin' back! Do I get nothing for all the pain and suffering? You were driving and I get hurt and you get all the money? How does that work, Sarah?"

I couldn't believe what he was saying. He was driving, we just said I was because the insurance wouldn't have paid up if he had been driving. I know my dad paid for anyone under 25 to be added to the policy but Marg says the insurance company wouldn't accept that and would only allow me as I was his daughter or something. I hadn't told this to my dad but I had checked the accounts and found Marg had paid the lower premium but there was no record of reimbursing Dad the $159 difference. But so what? That didn't give Stewart the right to say the insurance money was his, surely?

"I told you I would share it, lover. I mean I just got it yesterday in my account, alright?"

He looked a little calmer when I said that, took a half step back and I felt the air between us cool. He really was steamed up about this but I wasn't trying to keep his money from him. I really didn't know he was supposed to get any of it. I thought it was to replace my car and I said this to him as I squeezed past him into the living room.

"You still got your car, Sarah, remember? I fixed that up for you. You still got your car and you got the payout from the insurance company. I sorted that but it cost me money and I need reimbursing. I explained all this to you, remember?"

I remembered he talked me nearly unconscious about the insurance and how he could have the car assessed as a write off then buy back the wreck and fix it and have it back on the road. He said he had a mate and he could fix it all and I had given him the $500 he said it would cost. Plus I paid the $2,000 excess, all from my savings. I got the cheque from the insurance company for the $25,000 the car was covered for, so I guess I was up $22,500, plus as Stewart said, I still had the car. Well his mate had it. He loaned Stewart a shitbox we were getting around in now while he re-birthed it or whatever they called the process. All totally legit and legal, Stewart swore.

"How much do you need, lover?"

"How much did they pay you?"

"Well, I got the twenty five grand but I paid out two in excess first and then there was the five hundred I gave to you for your mate to do the assessing and stuff. Which reminds me, when do we get the car back and give him back that old heap of sh…"

"Don't friggin' worry about that, I told you I'll sort it. You got wheels for now and besides, we usually take my car everywhere, even if it is getting old."

He was going to go on about his car again, I could just tell. He had a 1992 Hyundai that was falling apart when I met him. I lent him the money to put down on a new car, well a new second hand car. It was a really sick Nissan Coupe, one of those turbo charged grey imports from Japan. When it went it went like stink, as his dad Nathan used to say. Trouble was it wasn't going much at all lately and getting parts was difficult and expensive. I really loved his car because I felt like I was his sexy partner in crime and we had just boosted the car and were running from the law like in the game he has on the X-Box, Gran Turismo or something.

"Well, lover, maybe we can get your car fixed? Use some of the money for those repairs, get it registered again and everything?" I know he was saying before how it was going to cost him five grand to get it road worthy and registered again and he didn't have the money, but now I had it and I'd happily give it to him as a present. Not a loan, I mean he's my boyfriend, you know, the father of our child and everything.

"Yeah, we could but then it's still a crappy old car, ain't it? We need a new car, lover. Especially with bubby coming along. Something bigger and safer. A bit of steel around you and the baby, ya know?"

How sweet! He was thinking of our safety. I had to admit the Nissan was pretty low down. I always worried about running under a truck when we parked behind one in traffic. "Yeah, lover, that would be cool. What did you have in mind?"

"Shane's got just the thing!" Shane was his mate who was arranging the re-birth of my car. "He says we can have this really cool Commodore, it's a 2005 model, almost brand new, ex-cop car, Highway Patrol, fully sick and everything. I mean they don't make them any safer than cop cars, right?"

"Yeah, course lover. So, how much does he want for this car?"

"He said he'll take your car as a trade in and fifteen grand."

"My car? You mean the…"

"Yeah. He says it might not be smart to get it back to you anyway, seeing as how they paid out on it and it should really be a write-off and all. Better he sells it interstate. Anyway, that and fifteen grand and you said you got twenty five, so what's the problem?"

"Well, what about your car? Aren't you trading that in on it?"

"Nah, he doesn't want it, too much to fix he says. I'll sell it privately but that will take time and this Commodore isn't going to sit around and wait forever for us."

"I don't know, Stewart, I mean I thought he was fixing my car and…"

"Fer chrissakes, Sarah! He's doing me a favour. Doing you a favour too, alright? If he hadn't taken your shit heap you would never have gotten it written off. They would have fixed it and you'd be driving around in a dodgy, dangerous half fixed car. With our kid in it! Is that all you think of our kid? C'mon Sarah, grow some, ok?"

I couldn't help it, I started to cry again. I was always just one eyeblink away from bursting into tears these days. I felt so selfish, thinking about my car and the money and then Stewart is only thinking of the safety of our baby and I just felt wretched.

"I'm sorry, Stewart. I don't mean to be selfish, I'm just confused, you know? That's why I need you, lover, I leave it all to you, ok? What do you want?"

He took me in his arms then. I nearly melted. He had been pretty distant since we'd had the argument over whether he was the father or not and everything. It had been pretty tense for a few days but it seemed everything was ok again. I was forgiven for making him angry with my stupid questions. I really should trust him and not question everything he does for us. He's right about how I really am not smart enough in the right way to follow all the angles as he calls them. He says I'm not dumb, just women are smart in different ways to men and these car things are bloke's business. Makes sense and besides, all I really care about is that he loves me and he loves our baby. I never saw my car again, or the fifteen grand I withdrew for the Commodore but I had to admit the new car was awesome. You could still see the holes where the radar and radios and stuff had been mounted, Stewart said. He pointed them out to me the day he picked up the new car from Shane. The thing went like stink, in fact it stunk more than the Nissan. That was Stewart' joke about the Commodore being faster than the old jap crap rice burner as he called it now. He still had it, sitting outside on the street, a 'For Sale' sign in the back window but no one had called about it. Not that we cared now we had a nice, safe family sedan.

We took it to the airport to pick up Mum and Dad when they came back from the UK. Dad was impressed, riding up the front with Stewart while I sat in the back and hugged mum all the way home. Stewart was on his best behaviour and we all seemed to settle down after a few tense moments when we first met in the Arrivals Hall. Mum kept looking at me but the bruising had disappeared enough to be hidden by my make up and besides, that was history now.

***

"It is gonna hurt, Sarah. I mean, really, really hurt. Like you are exploding down there."

"Stewart!" He was winding me up again, telling me how much having a baby was going to hurt. He was just teasing but it was starting to get to me. To be honest, I was scared. I had watched some YouTube videos and it looked really scary, painful and everything.

"But I'll be with you, Sarah. All the way. No matter how much it hurts, I'll be there for you, lover."

"I know you will sweetie but please, can you stop saying how much it will hurt. You're scaring me, Stewart."

"I'm just playing, lover. They give you drugs, epi-cure-alls and stuff. I read about it, or saw a video or something. You won't feel a thing. Once that bowling ball sized head passes through there… hahahahaha."

I had a mental vision of a bowling ball coming out and the nurse holding it up by the three holes and I nearly threw up. "Stewart! Don't!" He just laughed and went off to the bathroom. He'd been spending a bit of time in the bathroom lately. I hadn't asked why but he would stay in there for twenty minutes at a time, sometimes longer, the door locked and the bathroom radio on. I was curious as to why but I wouldn't dare ask in case he thought I was prying into his business.

He came out half an hour later and said we should go to the mall, just walk around a bit. I was feeling pretty tired but I didn't say so. Last time I had tried to get out of a mall trip I had made him angry and he had lost it again. I just didn't feel like walking around the shops and buying something for the sake of buying something when I was feeling so tired and run down. We went to the mall and walked around and he bought himself a shirt, well I bought it for him because he'd left his wallet at home, again. I didn't mind, he looked good in the shirt but I was a bit upset when he said he'd wear it on his next boy's night. I thought he'd wear it next time we went out, seeing as how I bought it. I said that, too.

Got the look. Or rather, 'the look'. I knew that look well enough to quickly tell him it was ok, he could wear it when he went out with his mates. We hadn't been out together for a couple of weeks anyway.

"I gotta drop by my old man, pick something up, ok?"

"Yeah, sure, lover. Let's go."

"Nah, I'll drop you home first. No point you traipsing over there for no reason. Besides, he might be in a bad mood about your dad ripping him off."

"My dad never ripped him off! He just pays on thirty days, he pays all his creditors on thirty days…"

"Yeah, well my dad's not a creditor. He's owed money for doing work for your dad."

I wasn't about to try and explain the meaning of 'creditor' as Stewart had no idea how the books are kept in a business. His dad was a creditor, or supplier of services and Dad pays all his suppliers on thirty days after invoice. In fact, he made an exception and let Marg pay Nathan every week like the employees but that seems to have been forgotten by Stewart. And Nathan. He wasn't doing any cleaning work for Dad now him and Mum were back in Brissie and I think he was pissed off about that. I guess Stewart was right not to take me, but then he changed his mind.

"Aw shit, I can't be bothered going all the way home then turning around and driving past the mall again. C'mon, you can come with me. Maybe just stay in the car, hey?"

Which suited me. I didn't like Nathan, to be honest. I couldn't figure out what Marg saw in him. I mean she was such a sweet woman and he was such a nasty bloke. I never said anything to Marg or Stewart, that would be stupid because they were his partner and his son and everything. I hadn't said anything to Dad or Mum, either. Just kept it to myself like I keep just about everything. I keep too much stuff bottled up inside, I think. I know one day I'll explode but what can I do? Stuff about Stewart I can't tell Mum or Dad or they'll say 'I told you so' and want us to break up and I love him. He's the father of my kid. They don't understand him like I do. If they did then they'd be different, I know. I can't tell Marg, she'd go straight to Mum or Nathan or worse, Stewart. I dunno about Marg. I love her like a second mum sometimes but sometimes… Sometimes there is like this veil that comes down across her eyes and it's like talking to someone completely different.

Stewart parked the Commodore outside his dad's house. Actually it was Marg's place from her previous divorce and Nathan moved in with her. It was a traditional Queenslander with a bullnose verandah and raised on stilts with an open deck underneath. There was an old punching bag hanging up and a couch that had seen better days, some boxes and a few stacked plastic patio chairs and a portable gas BBQ. All pretty neatly stacked around the space beneath the house. I knew inside the house it would be tidy, too. Marg was a tidy person, as tidy a person as Nathan was a slob. If she let him get away with it he would be lying on the couch surrounded by empty XXXX beer cans and pizza boxes, chip packets and the like. He was pretty lazy, slovenly my mum would call it.

I stayed in the car and Stewart went in for a few minutes, then came out and beckoned to me from the verandah. I got out and walked up the steps, asking half-way; "Whaddya want?"

"Marg says come inside, she's making coffee. Did you lock the car?"

I hadn't so I went back and locked it manually as Stewart had the keys. He could have hit the central locking from where he was but he said he'd left the keys inside on the coffee table so I guess it was easier for me to just walk back and lock up. This wasn't a bad area as such but you didn't want to take any chances, as Stewart always said. I mean how embarrassing if you had an ex-cop car and it got pinched and all because you forgot to lock it, right?

When I made it into the lounge Marg was putting the coffees down on the coffee table, Nathan was taking up the three seater couch and Stewart had the other armchair. I could have sat in the one, free armchair but that was Marg's seat so I just perched on the arm of Stewart' chair. I sipped my coffee and didn't say anything, not wanting to set Nathan off or make any trouble for Stewart or Marg. I finished my coffee after a few exchanges with Marg while Stewart and Nathan talked about something to do with cars, then I picked up my cup and Marg's and took them into the kitchen.

"That's alright love, I can do that" said Marg rather hastily.

"No, it's alright, Marg, I don't mind" and I was half way into the kitchen anyway. I took another two steps and I was in the kitchen proper and looked around for a place to set the cups down as the sink was pretty much overflowing. I saw there was a Zip water boiler on the wall, a new one, just like the one Dad had put into the lunch room at work. That thing had cost him a fortune, he was stunned, he'd said, how much the convenience of on tap boiling water cost. Marg had sworn she'd hunted around the internet for the best deal, taken care of everything for him as it had been while he was away.

"You got a Zip like the one at work, Marg" I remarked. I mean it was silver, shiny and stuck on the wall for all to see, you couldn't fail to mention it.

"Oh yeah. Got that the other week, a real time saver."

"It looks like the same model we got at work last month."

"Not quite, this is the smaller one. Domestic. We got the industrial version, much more expensive. I got a deal on this because the same bloke fitted it as did the one in the lunch room."

Marg seemed a bit embarrassed about having a Zip in her own kitchen but I know lots of people have them these days, saves a lot of time if you are always boiling water. "Oh, yeah, alright. I might get one when I have my own place. Me and Stewart, I mean." I guess our flat was my own place as Dad and Mum bought it for me and I barely paid any rent for it, but I still thought of it as a rental unit, not my own. I was thinking a house with a back yard and a garage for Stewart to keep the Commodore in and mess about in. That was what I thought of as my own place. Our place. Not a place Mum and Dad bought me. Well, maybe they could help us with the deposit but still, somewhere Stewart and I could call our own. I'd get a Zip then, for the baby formula and stuff.

"C'mon out onto the deck, let's leave the boys to their car talk, ok, Sarah?"

I followed Marg out onto the deck that joined the kitchen and laundry area. It had a patio dining set and another gas portable BBQ, this one was one of those big six burner jobbies with the wok burner and rotisserie. I was struck with how similar it was to one Dad bought for work last year. We used to have Friday arvo BBQs when the work was flowing. All the tradies and installation crews rocked up to drop off their work sheets for the week and would have a couple of cold beers or some softies and a steak sandwich. Dad paid for it all, just made sure nobody had more than two beers, light ones, since they were usually driving the company vans and utes home. Plus they all had a good feed of snags or steak and some salad. Dad said what it cost him in beer and meat he more than got back in loyalty and good work from the crews. He had a breathalyzer he bought from Dick Smith's and made sure all the driver's checked their blood alcohol levels before they left for the day. We hadn't run one for a few weeks, not since they were away, just not as much work on, or crews too busy or maybe just not the same vibe without Dad and Mum in the factory. Marg kept the business running but it wasn't the same as when Dad and Mum were here.

"I like your BBQ, Marg. It's huge!"

"Yeah, a present from Nathan last Christmas. I think he liked the one your dad got for the factory, bought it from the same mob, I think. Have a look at the view, not much but you can see the mountains over there and a glimpse of the sea that way."

She was right, it wasn't much of a view but between the houses surrounding hers you could catch a glimpse of the mountains to the west and the tiniest patch of darker blue sea under the sliver of light blue sky to the east. I forgot about the BBQ as Marg talked to me about this and that, just the usual small talk. I was actually relaxing and enjoying myself when Nathan came out onto the verandah and everything changed, once and forever. With just four words.

"You're a fucking slut!"

I Felt Like I Wanted To Die

"It was horrible, Mum." I was having a cup of coffee with my mum and it felt so good to be back home. Dad was out playing golf but he'd be back before I had to go back *there*. I couldn't bring myself to call my flat home. "Now Stewart is saying we should move in with Marg and Nathan, to save money for the baby and all."

"You don't have to do that, pet. I'll talk to your dad, I'm sure if the rent is getting too much for you he'll give you some wriggle room. You know your dad, softest touch in Surfer's!"

I laughed at that, Mum was right. My dad was the softest touch in Surfer's, at least for his family and those he trusted. Anyone else had to stand in line and when it came to business he could be as hard-nosed as the best of them. If he could reduce the rent, even though we paid well under market rate as it was, that would help.

"I don't know why, Mum, but we never seem to have any money these days. I mean I pay the rent and the electricity and the food from my pay, even put petrol in Stewart' tank and the other night he took $50 from me purse for his boy's night out."

"He did what?" Mum sounded pretty concerned so I played it down.

"Well, he borrowed it, he'll pay it back, I'm sure. I mean…"

"Sarah, when they start 'borrowing' from your purse, then asking if it is ok… he did ask, right?"

I nodded. He hadn't asked at all, just told me when I asked him the next day if he knew what happened to the fifty dollar note I had in my purse. He hesitated, I saw him. He was going to lie, I know. He didn't though. He just said he was short and he knew I wouldn't mind. Came over all sweet and sugary but that's starting to get old these days. Since he hit me. Since his dad called me a slut.

"Still, I don't think it's right, pet. He's supposed to be the one supporting you and the wee one. Instead you're supporting him. What's he do with his money?"

"His car, mostly. He says it needs some work. A new computer chip last week. That was a grand. Then he changed the headers, whatever they are. And the suspension. Said the cop suspension was too soft for the power of the engine. Well his mate Shane said it and he just takes everything that guy says about cars and gives him his money. It's a lovely car but…"

"But it's just a car, love. You can't eat it and you'd soon get sick of living in it, so he should stop spending his wages on that and contribute more to the shared expenses. I mean, what if you were married? Man and wife and all? Then he'd…"

"Mum! Let's not get started on the marriage trip again, ok? Please?" My mum had this thing about getting married and I agreed with her completely, well almost. I wanted to be Mrs Stewart Lethbridge but I knew nagging Stewart would be the surest way of scaring him off. He had made it clear the night he thumped me I had to change a lot for the good before he would even consider thinking about marrying me and being tied down to someone like me. That's what he said and at the time it made sense but to be honest, I'm not so sure now. I mean I've been thinking and I don't think it is all my fault. I'd love to talk to Mum about it but she'd just go off with one of her old fashioned rants about decent blokes and what they do and how there aren't many like my dad left and all that. All very good but dad was already taken and I wasn't going to even think about that. Stewart was a good man. Mostly.

"Alright then pet but seriously, you need to take stock of your life now you have a bubby on the way. The first one is always the scariest because you don't know what it will be like. You can talk to me and every other woman who has had kids but nothing prepares you for the real thing. It really is very, very personal and even if Stewart is there holding your hand that is still a journey you have to take all by yourself. Just you and baby."

Mum was right, of course. No matter who was in the delivery room with me it would be just me and the baby going through all that pain and suffering. I was scared, I admit, but I was excited too. It was exciting, yet frightening at the same time, all adrenalin and what have you. I felt like that moment when Nathan called me a fucking slut, scared but excited, ready to fight or run away. I told mum what he had said and she was livid.

"He had no right! I mean, what the hell was he going on about? How could he call you a… a… that!" Mum stood up and strode to the jug in two steps, slammed the button down and sent the kettle boiling, just like her anger. I could see she was getting worked up about this. I hadn't wanted to upset her but I needed to tell her, tell someone and I knew if I told dad then he would be off out the door and screaming over to Nathan's and who knows what would happen then. I had timed my moment right, I thought. Just as mum finished giving me all that advice about the journey you took on your own I just blurted it out.

"Nathan called me a 'fucking slut', Mum." That had stunned her. Before she could ask for the details I began filling them in, telling her about that night and what happened after he had abused me. "He just walked in and said that and Stewart didn't say a word! I couldn't believe it. I asked him what did he mean and he said I knew and I should be ashamed of myself and that in his day if a slut tried to trap a decent bloke with that old 'I'm pregnant bullshit' she got what was coming to her."

Mum had grabbed my arm across the table and said, "he didn't hit you, did he, pet?"

"No, but I thought he was going to. He said in the old days all it took was 'one good upper cut to the slut's belly and it didn't matter who was the friggin' father'." Mum went pale at that. Literally went white.

"The bastard! He didn't. Did he?"

"Yes, Mum. He was right in my face and I could smell the rum on him and he was spitting saliva as he yelled at me and I looked at Stewart and he did nothing and then Marg told him to calm down and he turned on her and gave her lip about how I was a slut and trying to trap his son and he wouldn't let it happen. I thought he was going to punch me and kill my baby."

"So what did you do? What did you do then, pet?"

"I ran out of the kitchen and just kept going, out the front door and into the street. I heard him yelling behind me about how he would sort me out and Marg said to be quiet or the whole street would hear him and then Stewart came out and I told him I wanted to go home." It had been quite a scene. I was crying my eyes out and I was so scared Nathan would kill my baby.

"What did Stewart say then, love?"

"He said I should come back inside and stop carrying on. He said it was obvious Nathan was just drunk and didn't know what he was saying. I didn't agree, I told him I was not going back inside and I wanted to go home and he said too bad we're staying. Then he just left me there on the front fence and went back inside."

"Ahh, love. What did you do?"

"I went home. Stewart must have forgotten I had the car keys because he said he was going to get drunk and I could drive him home, seeing as how I wasn't drinking since I was pregnant. So I just drove off, did a burn out and nearly went sideways into some neighbour's car!" Mum and I laughed at that. "It was funny Mum, but I nearly wet myself. That is a very powerful car and I learned right then and there never to run from the police, they *will* catch you."

"That's what your dad always says. They're trained to drive them fast, too. So what happened next then?"

"Well I got home and went inside and the phone was ringing and it was Stewart and he was so angry and said I had to come back to the party or else. I asked him what did 'or else' mean and he just said I better come back and that if I didn't he would report me for stealing his car!"

"He didn't!"

"He did, Mum. He said I didn't have his permission to drive off like that and I told him he gave me the keys and he said that was for later, after the party and not then. I just said he could stay at his dad's for the night, I didn't want him home anyway."

"What did he say to that? I bet he wasn't happy about you telling him where to get off like that."

"Yeah, no, I mean he wasn't happy. He went off, said his dad was right, I was a slut and it wasn't his kid and he'd sort it. I was so scared I was trembling. I wanted to hang up but I thought if I did it would make him worse and besides, while he was on the phone I knew where he was and he wasn't there with me. You know?"

Mum nodded and made another cuppa for both of us and I could see she was upset by it all. She sat down and took my free hand in hers and then brushed the hair from my eyes with her other hand just as she had when I was a kid. I felt about twelve years old and it felt nice but I know I'm not a kid anymore and I have to work out my own problems.

"So what did you do then?"

"I left his car keys on the table and took mine and got in my car and went for a drive. I didn't want to be home when he arrived, if he came home that night, and I didn't want to be there the next morning either. I dunno, I just wanted to get away, get some space and time to think, you know?"

"I do, pet, I do."

"I drove around and then I parked in the Macca's carpark, you know the 24 hour one on the highway?"

"Yeah."

"So I went in, had a coffee, read the papers, used the free wi-fi and just hung out. Then I had breakfast and went for another drive and that's when I found myself in the driveway, just as dad disappeared round the corner. I figured he'd be playing golf this morning so we'd have the time together. I love dad but, well, I just don't want him going off, you know?"

"I do, you're right, love, your dad would've grabbed his five iron and gone round there this very morning and who knows where that would've ended. I think it best we keep this between us girls for the moment, till we figure out what you're going to do and once the tempers die down a little. OK?"

"Yeah, OK. Is it alright if I…"

"Of course, pet, love to have you. You know where your room is, or have you forgotten already?" We laughed together again. It was good to be home. I knew I couldn't stay forever and I'd have to face Stewart sooner or later. But not then and there. Not that day and not until I was good and ready. I was home and I was safe, he couldn't hurt me or my baby here. Our baby.

When Dad came home after his 18 holes and a few light beers on the 19th he was in a jovial mood, looking forward to his Sunday lunch. He was glad to see me and I guess the look mum gave him warned him not to ask any questions so he was keeping his curiosity in check all through lunch. We were all sitting on the back deck, enjoying the sunshine and warm weather, sharing the roast chicken and salad mum had whipped up after a quick trip to the supermarket deli counter and we were having a great old family chin wag. I remember thinking how lovely it was, all of us sitting here and how even nicer it would be when our babies were born. My new baby brother or sister and my own, first born child. Hopefully Stewart would be sitting here too, enjoying the family get-together. It was right at that very moment I thought of Stewart sharing the memories with us that he appeared. Our house backs onto the canal and there he was, tying up a small runabout at our little jetty, then striding across the back lawn, past the glass fence of the pool and across the pavers to the steps leading to the deck. Dad had his back to the canal and Mum was half looking past me into the house so it must have been the look of sheer horror on my face that made them turn, just as Stewart reached the table and spat out, "You're coming home! NOW!"

Part Four – Stewart

I Love Her, But…

"She stole ya fuckin' car? Strewth! Sort the bitch out, Stewart, ferchrissakes!" Dad was pretty pissed off. Pissed too, pretty much off his face which for him means he had been drinking a lot. Since this morning in fact. He did that most days, but all day and all night on the weekends when he didn't have to work. Work was not something he did everyday as it was, so he had plenty of days to get stuck into the grog. He could hold it, though, I give him that. But tonight he was not doing as well as some nights and I guess that's why he went off at Sarah.

"Well, she did have the keys, dad. I mean she was the desecrated driver."

"Designated, Stewart. She was the designated driver, not desecrated." Marg was always correcting me, as if she was some kind of university professor. 'The Grammar Nazi' Dad called her, sometimes. He read that on Facebook and figured it fitted her, the way she was always correcting both of us. At home anyway, never at work. Two totally different people, she was. The Marg they saw at work was all efficiency and sweetness. The one we copped at home was a bitch. Plain and simple. She was a control freak, it's why I was so keen to move out, even if I couldn't really afford it. Luckily Sarah's dad let us have their flat cheap.

"Whatever. I don't even know what you're talking about but you know what I meant. So why friggin' correct me? Why play 'Grammar Nazi' all the time, huh?"

"You watch your mouth, son, or I'll put my friggin' fist in it! Don't you talk to your mother like that!"

"Step-mother" corrected Marg but too late. I was already firing back at dad. I was like that, a bit hot tempered and quick to go off. So was Dad.

"She's not me fuckin' mother, alright?"

"Don't fuckin' swear in front of her, you little shit!"

That had both me and Marg stumped for a second, then we just pissed ourselves laughing. We couldn't help it.

"Whatcha friggin' laughing about, youse two?" Dad was standing there with his mouth wide open, looking from me to Marg and back again. He couldn't see the funny side of what he just said, which didn't surprise me. He doesn't have much of a sense of humour, Dad. Not the sharpest tool in the shed, my mum once told me. My real mum, not Marg. Well, if she told me once she would have told me a thousand times and she was right but at least he wanted me in his life these days. I remember when it was just me and mum for so long and I never heard from him. I think he was in prison but he denies that and so does mum, so who knows?

"Never mind, Nathan. Sit down and I'll get you another Bundy and coke. Stewart. Ring her up. She'll be home by now." Marg was being bossy Marg again but if it kept dad under control I didn't mind. I could see he was like two steps away from doing something stupid. I swear I thought he was going to punch Sarah in the gut right then and there. He had that look in his eye, the look he got when he used to give Mum a bit of a going over. She deserved it he said and she never really said she never so maybe she did. Women need it sometimes. Dad told me that years ago, before I even started going with Sarah. Sometimes sheilas forget themselves and just need a love tap, remind them who's boss and all. That's what dad says and I know he done it to Marg a few times. She hit him back, or first, or both but she knew she deserved it and besides, she was still with him so something had to be right between them.

"Sarah. It's me. Yeah. Bring the fucking car back. Now!" I flicked the phone to speaker so the others could hear what she was saying.

"No. I'm not going back there. Nathan said he was going to kill our baby!"

"No I fucking never…"

"Shut up Nathan!"

I covered the phone while Marg dragged Dad back onto the settee and put her hand over his mouth to keep him quiet.

"Look, Stewart, tell them… can they hear me? Have you got this on speaker? You prick! This is personal, Stewart. Between you and me. Not them!"

"Just bring the friggin' car back right now, ok? Bring it back now or else!"

"Or else what?"

"Or else I'll report it to the police that you stole my car! That's friggin' what else. Alright?"

"Stole it? You gave me the key, you moron!"

"Oy! I gave you the key because I was going to have a few drinks and you were the desecrat… I mean designated driver. Not so you can piss off and do burnouts up the bloody street in my car on my tyres!" I was about to add 'bitch!' when she flew back at me down the line.

"Your tyres? I paid for the, I paid for the whole friggin' car. What about…"

"Aw, I fuckin' knew you'd throw that back in my face. Typical. Fucking typical!"

"Typical? You little prick!"

And so it went on and she wasn't bringing the car back no matter what I said. She had a point about paying for the car but how low is that? You offer to help your boyfriend, the father of your kid, or so she claims, and then you throw it in his face all the time. Why bother? She was being a bitch. An ungrateful bitch. I mean I bought that car for her and the kid. So's they'd be safer than my old one. Shane was right, women don't appreciate cars and they don't appreciate doing them a favour. Treat them mean and keep them keen!

"I'll be there in five minutes and you'd better have the car and it had better have all its rubber and no dings!"

"Don't you dare come here tonight! I don't want you anywhere near me."

"I'll be there when I want to be there and you'd better be ready to do your conjugal job." I'd read that conjugal word somewhere. Meant a woman had to put out for her bloke if they were together and having a kid and living in the same flat is about as together as it gets.

"Piss off Stewart Lethbridge. You're getting nothing off me tonight and if you don't stop being a prick, you never will get anything else."

"Listen, bitch! You bring that fuckin' car back now or I'll fuckin' sort out that bastard baby of yours myself!" I didn't mean it but I was pissed, too. Pissed off at her attitude and disobedience and pissed as a fart. Well, too pissed to risk driving which meant I wasn't that pissed because I could still figure that out for myself.

"Bastard!" Click…brrrrrrrrr.

"She fucking hung up on me! On me! The bitch hung up on me!"

"I'm not surprised, Stewart. You catch more flies with honey than vinegar and you were pissing vinegar all over the place. She was scared of you, you idiot."

"Don't call me an idiot, Marg, I'll…"

"You'll what? Punch me in the gut, too? That's your dad's job!" She laughed as she said this and just turned on her heel and walked off into the kitchen.

"She's a tough one, son, our Marg. That's why I have to give her a love tap from time to time. Keep her in line or else she'd take over. Her kind always do. Or they try. You gotta know your woman and how to control her. Your Sarah, she's dumb as dog shit and not half the woman Marg is. You should be wrapping her round your little finger but instead she's telling you to piss off. C'mon, son. Get a friggin' grip and get her sorted!"

He was right. She was walking all over me. If I let her get away with that this time, she'd try it every time and before you know it she'd make me do something to get meself thrown in jail for. Wouldn't be my fault but the way the soft-cock courts looked at things these days, as dad too often reminded me, well I'd get crucified. She had been fine until she got pregnant, then went all holier than thou and mature on me. I gave her a tap to put her in her place and that seemed to work but I figure she's been talking to that bitch mother of hers. Or her dad. He was alright but a typical pommy. Dad said that too, right after Adam ripped him off. Not paying him for all the work dad did saving his business and all, well no wonder the mother and daughter behaved like they do. Shit I was tight! Too much Bundy, not enough coke.

"Stewart." It was Marg, standing over me like some middle aged MILF cougar whatever they called them. Looking leery and not what I would consider worth screwing, but Dad was no Tom Cruise either, so I suppose they were a good match.

"Huh?" I was nodding off, so pissed I could hardly stay awake.

"Sleep it off tonight. Tomorrow she will be at her parent's place. Check your flat first, she will probably leave the keys there and take her car. If she has, get your car and go round and tell her to come home."

"What if she won't let me in? They got that huge security gate and the internet thing."

"Intercom. It's called an intercom. Nevermind. They changed the code when they came back from Pommy Land so I don't know what it is to open that gate." She paused for a moment, deep in thought. "I know! Go in via the canal! You can take Nathan's tinny, launch it at the ramp down the canal from their place and tie up at their jetty. Nothing to stop you. Just walk across the back lawn, past the pool and in through the patio. I doubt they lock the sliding door off the deck. You know her room. Go in and just tell her you're there to take her home. Be nice. Can you manage that?"

"Huh? Yeah. Alright. Tomorrow." That was it for me. I just let go and went to sleep. I'd deal with the bitch tomorrow. Of course, when tomorrow came, I was still pretty pissed off but no longer really angry. Actually I don't mind saying I was starting to feel a little apprehensive about doing this. Not scared, of course, just a little bit unsure. I mean, who knows what Adam might do? Call the cops, pull out a shotgun, you never know with blokes like him. All straight up and a good bloke most of the time but if you piss them off. My dad says he's a moron, a pommy wanker and that, but I always liked Adam. He did the right thing by me but as dad says, honour is honour and that daughter of his dissed me in front of my dad and Marg and if she wants to be with me then she needs to know her place. That's what dad says and he would know, he's had lots of missuses. Not just Mum or Marg, but four or five he's lived with long term. Every one dissed him and every one he sorted out, usually with a back hander and then just walking out.

"If they give you mouth and grief over borrowing a few bucks from their purse so a man can have a drink with his mates after a hard day's work, then they ain't worth having, ya know?" Dad had said this years ago, more than once. I remember the last time we had this conversation, right after I put the phone down to Sarah.

"Whaddya mean, Dad?"

"Well, it's simple, son. Woman is on this earth to serve man, says so in the Bible."

"I didn't know you were religious, Nathan," said Marg. She was in the kitchen fixing a snack but could hear us, of course.

"It's nothing to do with religion, pet. It's the Bible."

I could hear Marg's gears whirring as she mulled over this gem of Dad's the same as I was doing. I was going to ask him to clarify but thought better of it. So, too, did Marg. Dad carried on almost right away, anyway.

"You find it in all the religious books. The Bible, the Torana, the Korana, the one the Hindu's read; all of 'em."

"What's the 'Torana', Dad?" I knew what he meant but I like to pull his chain now and then.

"The Torana, the Jew book, you know, the Jewish Bible. And the ragheads got the other one, the Korana. The one they get all pissed off about if you burn the thing, you know."

"Ah, yeah, I remember now. I used to call them the Torah and the Koran. Thanks for correcting me. I'd have felt an idiot if I'd got that wrong in an argument." I was pushing it but he was so drunk I doubt he'd know I was taking the piss.

"You're welcome."

Marg came in with some nachos she'd whipped up and we set on it like a pack of hungry dogs. I was still pretty pissed but sobering up and wondering if going around was the right thing afterall.

"You make sure you tell that little slag of yours to give your car back and she better sort her ideas out. If she wants to be a part of this family, anyways. OK? Stewart, you gotta start out as you mean to go on and that means she needs to know who wears the trousers and it's not her. Right?" Dad gave me that look I remember from my childhood, the look he used, even if pissed, to make sure you knew he was serious. Punch you in the face full on even if you are a woman or twelve years old serious.

"Yeah, Dad. Tomorrow, for sure." Shit. I was committed now. No turning back because he then nailed the coffin shut.

"Yeah, I'll come with you. Help you launch the tinnie. I might even drive it, save you having to mess around tying up when you hit their jetty. In and out quick like those US Navy WHALEs."

"SEALs, Dad. They're SEALs, not WHALEs. I saw a docco on them on Fox TV. Sea, Air Land. SEALs."

"Whatever. Bunch of pansy yanks. In and out like the SAS." He said is like sass, not S.A.S. That was my dad, always said and done things his way and everyone else was wrong. No point correcting him. He'd just come up with some other put down or excuse. Still, might be good having him with me tomorrow for a bit of moral support. Then again, it might be a friggin disaster.

She'll Be Back

"So, what happened?"

"Yeah, what happened? Did you snot the bastard?"

"No, Dad, I didn't snot the bastard. It got pretty heated but nobody got snotted, ok?" I was not really in the mood to go into a blow by blow, not that there had been any blows. In fact, it was pretty civilized. "I dunno, I walked across their lawn and they were right there, on the back deck, having breakfast. Sarah looked like she'd seen a ghost and I…"

"I bet she pissed herself!"

"No, Dad, she was just frightened, I guess. Understandable after everything she went through last night."

"Sounds like you rolled over and let her tickle your tummy like a piss weak puppy!"

"Bullshit! No, it wasn't like that. I mean, I felt bad when I saw how scared she was. Adam stood up and came towards me saying I should calm down. I guess I was pretty tense but I was angry. I just wanted me car back, y'know?"

"So what happened, Stewart?" Marg was sounding pretty cool. I think she knew what happened. Basically I had blubbered like a kid, but I wasn't telling them that. I wasn't telling them anything they would just turn and use to make me feel useless like they always did. The pair of them did it to each other. Dad used to do it to Mum. I didn't want that shit on top of everything else.

"Adam and me talked, and then Sarah and me talked and we sorted it out. I got me car back. Adam drove me to our place to get it. It's in the drive."

"I know it's in the drive, I heard you pull up. Hard to miss. So what did they say?"

"I bet the prick tried to blame it all on me, didn't he?"

"No, Dad." I was beginning to sound like an echo or a broken recording or whatever Dad called it when you repeated yourself. "I told them about last night and we agreed to work it out. Sarah's coming home tomorrow, just wants some time with her mum. That's cool with me. I mean, she's pregnant with my kid and everything."

"So it's your kid again, is it?"

"It's always been my kid, Dad. I'm going for a drive, I'm not putting up with your shit, just not in the mood, alright?"

You didn't mind putting up with my shit last night when I sorted that bitch out for ya? You didn't mind putting up with my shit when I took you to the jetty in my tinnie. Had to put the thing away meself, I got tired waiting for you. Go on, then, piss off!"

I didn't bother arguing with him any more, just walked out and went for a drive. Clear my head, you know? I was feeling pretty ashamed of myself, and Dad. The way we went after Sarah and all. I was pissed, so was he but that's no excuse, as Adam said. I know now, I have responsibilities. I'm going to be a father. I have to get it together. He was right with everything he said and the next day Sarah come home and we had great make-up sex and I just stayed away from Dad's and Marg's for a few weeks. Everything settled down and I went back to work for a while but my back wasn't up to it so I went on compo. That made it a bit strained between us as Sarah was still helping out at the office and Adam wasn't too happy about me being on compo but I couldn't work. Well, I could but fuck it! I'd had enough of that shit anyway. I figured I would take it easy for a while and then look for another job once the compo pay out came through.

***

"Christ Sarah! Nothing's been done! The place is a shit fight! No dinner ready, nothing been washed or ironed and I'm going out and where's my good shirt? In the friggin' wash! What the hell do you do all day? Sit around doing stuff all, that's what!" I was pissed off. Sarah was due any day now but that was no excuse. Christ, as Marg said, she's pregnant not friggin dying of cancer. Why the hell couldn't she do something around the house, it was a pigsty!

"Well where have you been all day, no, all friggin' week? Out looking for a job? My arse! You haven't looked for a job since you went on compo. You can work, you're just bullshitting. Anyone with a bad back can't screw…"

"Shut your fucking trap, you bitch! I've been… it's none of your friggin' business where I've been, ok? I'm not the one sitting at home doing nothing, alright?" No, I was down the pub with my mates doing nothing but screw her. I mean, compo is hard on a man's self esteem, Dad said that plenty of times and he would know. No self esteem and no work and no bloody compo but at least he had a good woman. Marg took care of him and didn't bitch and moan like Sarah. Even when he gave her a love tap she either hit him back or just copped it. She was the perfect woman for him. I used to think Sarah was the perfect woman for me but how wrong can you be?

"We haven't paid rent in three months. I'm due to give birth in two days and I cant cope and I get no support from you…"

"What do you want me to do, go to the shitter for ya?"

"You could clean up around here, it's mostly your bloody mess. Yours and your mates, coming around and bonging on. I'm fucking pregnant and your mates are smoking dope. You know the baby cops all that?"

"Bullshit. You piss off and hide in your room anyway. Or you run to your mummy. How much smoke can you cop there?"

"That's not the point. But then you never get the point, do you?"

"What the hell's that supposed to mean?"

"Forget it. I'm going to bed."

And off she stormed. Typical. It had been like this for weeks. She had gone off the rails. Not all at once, but bit by bit. It had been fine the first two weeks she came back after she stole the Commodore. Then she started to slip back into her old ways. Her mum's ways more like. Expecting me to do everything for her. Fer chrissakes what does she think I am? Her little black boy or summat? I'd told Dad and Marg and they said not to put up with her shit, basically. Let her know who was the man in the house and make it work. Easier said than done with that bitch. I was ready to toss her out but she was so close to having the kid and I confess I was curious what it would be, a boy or a girl. We'd had the ultrasound and all but since I didn't go with her she was being a bitch and not telling me. I had other things that day and besides, how friggin' hard is it to drive to the hospital and go and get the ultrasound. I'd gone for the first one but the ultra sound woman said she couldn't see whether it was a hotdog or a hamburger. Boy or girl she meant. She thought that was funny. I just thought it had better be a boy or I was going to be pissed off. Enough whining women in my life without making one of me own, ya know?

"If you can't be bothered to come with me, you can't be bothered to know."

"I'm the father, it is my right to know!"

"You're the father, it is your duty to be there with me, for me!"

"Duty? You been listening to your bloody dad carry on again, haven't ya? Bloody pommy bastard, who does he think he is?"

"He's a better man than you, Stewart Lethbridge. He took me to the ultra-sound. Did your job for you."

I was going to say something else about him doing 'my job for me' but I figured it would backfire, so I let it go. It wouldn't have mattered if I had said anything else as she'd already pissed off and locked herself in the bedroom. Stayed there all night so I slept on the lounge. She'd already gone to work the next morning so we never finished that argument, but it didn't matter as we went straight into the next one when she came home that night. That was how it had been now for I forget how long. I couldn't wait for the kid to pop out; hadn't had sex for weeks. Well, not with Sarah but I had a little action going with this chick I met at the pub. Nothing serious, just getting the laundry done, if you know what I mean. A man's got needs, as Dad says. I didn't cop any of the attitude with her, just did it in the car, she loved the new leather seats I'd scored off Shane. He took them out of a SS 317 he'd been wrecking and I got them for next to stuff all. Of course, Sarah went off about those.

"Where'd you get the money for these seats? We need every cent for…"

"I know, for the friggin' baby. You keep reminding me. In fact you never bloody stop. We get five grand from the government for having the baby. These cost just five hundred. I mean, do you now how much leather seats from a SS cost? Five hundred, that's like stealing them."

"You got them from Shane, they probably are stolen."

"He was wrecking a car been in a prang, alright?"

"That's what they do at chop shops, Stewart. They wreck cars for parts and sell them off to idiots like you. What if the cops…"

Which is when I lost it. She just pushed me over the edge, ya know? I'd taken this shit from her for months and I just snapped. I gave her a tap, just a tap and she starts howling like I'd cut her tits off or summat.

"Bastard! That's it! I'm going!"

"Well friggin' go then, useless bitch." I let her go. Good riddance. She'd come crawling back once she came to her senses. She'd be all lovey dovey and crawling up my arse. She stormed off into the bedroom, slammed the door behind her then came out five minutes later with her bag and just stormed out.

"What, just like that?" I was telling Marg about it the next day. She'd heard some version of events at work no doubt and wanted to get the true story.

"Didn't even slam the front door, just left it wide open. I heard her start her shitbox and drive off."

"Yeah, good riddance. Better off without her. Get someone in who'll take better care of you, son." Dad was being pretty supportive. He was sober, which always helped but today he seemed more friendly than usual.

"I couldn't give a stuff. I'd had it with her and her baby this and baby bloody that. Screw her." I laughed at that. I had. Screwed her I mean.

"No argument there, the proof was in the pudding. Pudding. Pudding Club, get it?" Dad was being his usual funny self and we all just laughed.

"She'll be back, Stewart. Once she's had the baby she'll realise she needs a man to support her. Her man, the father of her kid. You. She'll be back." Marg went to make the coffee. She was right, as usual. Sarah'd be back.

It's A Girl!

"You better get yourself to the hospital, Stewart."

It was Adam. He'd called me to tell me Sarah was in labour. She was having the baby right then and there. At three in the bloody morning. I had just got to bed, been down the pub with my mates. Got lucky with that little slut Emma in the Commodore and had a few bongs and too many Bundy's and coke. I was in no fit state to drive to the hospital. I'd pushed my luck far enough driving home from the pub but it was a Tuesday and the pub wasn't far. But the hospital was miles away.

"I'm too pissed to drive, Adam."

"Well get a taxi!" he sounded pissed off in that pommy way he has. I was ready to tell him to piss off when he spoke again.

"Look, I'll pay the cab when it gets here, just get your arse to the hospital. Sarah needs you and believe me, you'll hate yourself for life if you miss out on being there for your first born."

I was in the right mood to tell him to piss off and that I couldn't give a stuff, the kid was half hers and so would be half shit as it was but I was too pissed to care. So I hit the screen and ended the conversation. Screw him and screw his slag daughter. I'd go there tomorrow. Probably wait around for hours before the kid came out anyway. My cousin was in labour for eighteen hours with her first one. What the hell was I going to do for that long? Stare at the hole to see if it was coming?

Marg came into the kitchen looking like she was still asleep and that isn't a good look for someone her age. She sat down opposite and asked me who was on the phone. I told her it was her boss and his daughter was having a baby and he expected me to drive there after I told him I was too pissed.

"You gotta go, Stewart. You have to be there for the birth. You'll hate yourself if…"

"Christ, that's what he said. I don't think I'll hate myself for anything. Dad wasn't there for my birth, was he?"

"Well neither was I but it was different in those days. Nowadays it's expected the father will be at the birth. Go on, take a cab. I'll lend you the money."

"I'm too drunk, Marg. Besides, she will be in labour for hours. What's the rush?"

"Maybe she needs you, Stewart?"

"If she needed me why did she run out on me right before the baby was born, huh? Answer me that." Marg said nothing, just went and put the jug on and started making two cups of coffee.

"Make it three, love," Dad said as he staggered into the light of the kitchen. He looked worse than she did. What is it with people when they hit middle age? Just let themselves go I suppose. "What's going on?"

"Sarah's having the baby. Adam rang and told Stewart to get to the hospital, expected him to drive drunk!"

"Bloody typical of that man. Selfish bastard. No consideration for anyone else, just expects everyone to jump when he clicks his fingers. Why's Stewart gotta be there? Are the nurses on strike?" He laughed at his own joke but I was too far away to join in. I was beginning to have second thoughts. Maybe I should be there.

"I'll have my coffee and then maybe I'll go."

"Good for you, Stewart."

"What? What for, son? The kid'll be there tomorrow."

"No, he's right. He should go."

"Well you can see he's too pissed to drive. He'll lose his license or wreck his car. What was that pommy bastard thinking?"

"I'll get a cab, Dad."

"How much will that cost you? Fifty bucks? You haven't got fifty bucks."

"Adam said he'd…"

"He'd what?"

"Adam said he'd pay for the cab."

"Lend you the cab fare more like. And want it paid back tomorrow. With interest!" Marg was not in Adam's good books at the moment. She hadn't been for some time, not since he had almost accused her of cooking the books. The account books that is. Some bullshit about not paying the full insurance premium on Sarah's car, using money for inventory and all sorts of bullshit accusations. He'd had her in tears before he let up. That was last week and since then Marg hadn't a good word to say about him and I didn't blame her. You start calling people a thief and they are going to take offence, even if they have been a little liberal with the lolly, as I heard someone on TV say.

"I'll take you, son."

I looked at my dad. I was stunned. Not only for him offering, but the tone he used. It was almost, well, fatherly.

"Thanks Dad. We'll go after the coffee, yeah?"

"Yeah. Just give me a chance to use the shitter. Can't trust those hospital toilets. Full of golden staffies, y'know."

I looked at Marg and we shared a moment. Dad's forever getting his sayings mixed up but we never said anything. Most of the time it would just set him off and the rest he didn't have a clue what you were on about so he kept at it until he got angry and off he went. Now we just shared a look and laughed about it once he was out of the room.

"Here, drink this. Make you feel better. You're going to need your head together when you get to the hospital. Don't let those Clarkson buggers mess with your head."

"Thanks Marg," I said as I sipped at the coffee. "I think they've messed with it enough, don't you?"

"Yeah. Bastards."

***

"Thankyou, Mary", said Sue. Mary, once Lethbridge, now Stephens, is my mum. She married again a few years after Dad walked out. Her new bloke, I can never bring myself to call him my step-father, Ross, was a weedy little bastard. Worked for the taxman making other people's lives miserable. Marg despised him as much as I did, but for other reasons. He'd audited the factory once a few years ago and wasn't happy with what he found. Accused Marg of all sorts of rubbish before I'd walked into the office.

I remember asking him, "What are you doing here, Ross?"

"Oh, hello, Stewart. I'm working. Auditing the GST returns. Do you work here?"

Typical dumb question. What did he think I was doing in a t-shirt with the company name across my left tit? "Yeah. I do the installs. So, found all the skeletons in the closets then?"

He looked at me a bit sideways then with that glance he gives you sometimes when he is not happy. He never loses his cool, too small and weedy to take anyone on I guess. All the same, I didn't like the look he gave me but it was only there for a flash and then he smiled. He looked like a lizard, or a croc about to eat you.

"That's classified, as they say in the movies, Stewart."

"You two know each other, then?" Marg was also one for stating the obvious.

"Yes, Stewart is my step-son."

"Oh, yeah, that's where I had heard the name before, I thought it was familiar. I'm Stewart's step-mother."

"You married Nathan Lethbridge?" This was said with some incredulity, which is a word someone once used on me and I had to look it up.

"Well, common law wife. Partner. You know."

"Yes." There was more left unsaid in that one word response than if he'd have read out half of 'Lord of the Rings'. Marg had watched the exchange with some interest, probably figured she'd try and leverage the family connection. I just said my goodbyes and got the hell out of there. I'd only snuck in to see Sarah and she wasn't there so no point hanging around. I had only seen Ross about three times since then, family get-togethers on Mum's side mostly. I didn't see mum much these days as she'd moved away down south and any time I did see her I couldn't wait to piss off. Too many questions about this and that and when was I going to make something of myself. Much easier with Dad and I could see why he left, to be honest. I used to hate him for that but I was beginning to realise that living with Mum, in fact living with any woman, was hardly worth the benefits. I mean you can get your laundry done at the Laundromat for a few bucks, eat take-away if you can't cook and with sluts like that Emma around, why commit?

"I can't believe it, both of you having your babies almost side by side, well adjacent rooms, anyway." Mum was still going on, I guess women don't have much else to talk about. "Imagine, mother and daughter having babies at the same time."

"Yes, we think it is a good thing," said Sue.

"No, yes, I mean, it's wonderful," replied Mum, but she didn't seem that enthusiastic. I know in the car coming over she had said she thought it was ridiculous, a woman Sue's age having kids all over again and no way she'd do it. Then she went off on one of her lectures. Mum's a psyche nurse, well she's a nursing assistant in a mental hospital. Perfect place for her, Dad reckons and he might have something there. Mum's alright, she did her best bringing me up after Dad left but she does go on sometimes. But then what woman doesn't?

"Adam and I are rapt." Sue had picked up on Mum's tone, I think. She took the baby back and sat down on the sofa. We were all at Adam and Sue's place. This was the first time I'd been back since that morning Sarah stole my car. It was a kind of let bygones be bygones thing. Sarah had invited us all to come and see the babies and Marg had said we should and then we found out Sarah had called Mum and now here we all were. It was a bit tense at first but the babies seemed to soften everyone up.

"Here, Dad. Hold your daughter." Sarah gave me my daughter to hold and I very carefully took her, all wrapped up with nothing but her little face peeking out. "You won't break her, just don't drop her."

"Of course I won't drop her!" That came out a bit harsher than I intended but what is it with women? Always thinking us blokes are useless when it comes to anything domestic? I sat down on the seat across from Sue and we sat there holding our babies and everyone sat around and kind of looked at each other.

"So, Stewart, how does it feel being a father?" This was from Ross, who didn't have any kids so I guess he was curious.

"It's ok. I mean, it's great." Another dumb question. How would I know what it felt like to be a father? I hadn't been one for more than a few days and this was only the third time I'd seen the little bugger. I'd made it to the hospital just as the baby came out. That wasn't something I'd want to see again, to be honest. It was obviously bloody painful if the noise Sarah was making was any indication. I'd tried to comfort her, told her to ease up on the screaming and she screamed even louder!

"How'd you like it if I pushed a bowling ball out your arse?"

I'll never forget her saying that. She had this scrunched up face and sounded like one of those possessed women in the movies getting exercised or whatever they call it. She was all sweetness and light, now. Sitting there with a goofy look on her face as I held the baby. I have to admit that gets old fast and I was glad when she started to wail and Sarah took her back. Right there in front of everyone she just flopped out a tit and starting feeding her. She must have seen the look on my face because she said, "What? it's natural! Don't be such a prude, Stewart."

It might be natural but I didn't like Dad and Ross copping an eyeful of my woman's boob, with or without my daughter stuck to the end of it. "Yeah, but, in front of everyone?"

"It's alright, Stewart, we're all family now." Marg quickly stepped in to calm things down as always.

"Yes, well, er, yes. All family. Right." This was Adam. He'd just stepped into the room with the coffees on a tray. I don't think he thought of Marg as family, not anymore. He was still giving her grief over the books and I'd seen him having a quiet chat to Ross earlier, out on the back deck. Probably getting some tips on investigating fraud. By now I knew Marg was cooking the books. She'd been pissed the other night and boasted about it to me and Dad. She reckoned she'd taken him for ten grand already and there was more coming and he'd never find it, or prove it. I didn't give a toss, even if she was ripping off the father of the mother of my child. That was a mouthful. Easier to say Sarah's dad.

"So Adam, how's it feel, being a father again after all these years?" Bloody Ross again.

"I didn't know I'd stopped, Ross."

"Oh, yeah, sorry, I meant, being the father of a new baby after all these years."

"It feels great, Ross. Do you have any kids?"

Silence. Everyone was looking at Ross.

"Ross and I decided we wouldn't have any children, Adam." Mum coming to his rescue. "Ross's first wife and daughter were killed in a car accident and…"

"Oh, I'm sorry to hear that, really, sorry, Ross, I didn't know." Adam was back peddling like crazy, trying to dig himself out of that hole. I almost felt sorry for him, he looked genuinely upset. Then again, Ross looked pretty stunned too. I guess it was the fact Mum had just spouted a load of bullshit. Ross had never married before and from what I knew, couldn't have kids.

"I didn't know that, either, Ross," Dad chipped in. "I'd heard you were impudent."

I nearly laughed out loud. "You mean impotent, Dad."

"I'm very sorry to hear that too, Ross, forgive Nathan will you. He has no manners." Marg again, standing on Dad's foot and jumping in to smooth things over. "Coffee?" She began handing out the cups and in the confusion of making sure everyone got the right one the moment faded away.

We had the coffee, nursed the babies again, everyone taking a turn with both of the little buggers and then Dad and Ross and I started to make 'let's go and get a drink' noises. Well Dad and I did. Ross was just keen to get the hell out of there. The women of course dragged out the goodbyes and that left us blokes all milling around the car looking at each other and talking crap while they did the last minute fussing over the babies. It was a relief to start the car and drive off, everyone pretending we were 'family' and it had gone well. Which I guess it had, given the potential for disaster such a gathering brings.

"Well, that went well," said Mum.

"Yes, I thought so, too," said Marg. "It went well, didn't it, love?"

Dad just turned around and looked at her. She was in the middle seat with Mum on one side and Ross on the other. I figured she did that instinctively to place herself in the middle of the action, so to speak. "Yeah, right enough. Now how about we get a drink? One glass of that shampoo stuff to wet the babies' heads hardly did anything. I need a real drink. C'mon, go to the pub, Stewart."

"We'll pass, thanks, Nathan," said Ross. "Just drop us back at your place and we'll be off back home. They'd left their car at our house as they didn't know the way and Marg figured it would be better if we all rocked up together so we were in the Commodore.

"Yeah, alright then. Home, Stewart!" Dad said that in a posh pommy accent like I was the chauffeur and he and I laughed. It was an old joke but it never got old for us, always made us laugh. We dropped Mum and Ross off, her and Marg going on about babies for another ten minutes while Ross sat in his Citroen and checked his email on his iPhone. I hit the horn a few times but it didn't speed them up. Finally they did the air kiss thing and Marg got in and I drove off. Couldn't wait to hit the beer garden.

"So, when is she moving home, Stewart? Her and the baby." Marg had let me get half of my first beer down before she started up. I took another long pull on my beer before I answered. She wouldn't like what I was going to say.

"She's not sure, Marg. Says she wants to get settled with the new baby at her mum's for a while, first. Says she'll be home when she's ready." And not before is what she actually said, but I wasn't repeating that. Might make me look like I'd lost control.

"I see." There was a lot left unsaid in that 'I see'. She didn't wait long though. "So has she registered the baby in your name?"

"Not yet. We are going to talk that through before she submits the paperwork to Births, Deaths and Marriages." In fact she had said she wanted the baby to have my name, but that depended on whether we were getting back together. I was stunned. Of course we'd be getting back together. Until I said we weren't and told her to pack her bags. I decided that shit, not her!

"Sounds like she's running the show, now, Son. See, that's what happens when you go soft on them and let them run home to mummy and daddy!" Dad was winding up, I could tell.

"Nah, Dad, she's just upset, after all that's happened and all, that's all."

"And all and all and all," Dad mimicked me. "Jeez, you sound like an Irish parrot." He thought that was so funny he was too busy laughing to say something else, so Marg jumped in. As always.

"You need to take control, Stewart. Get the kid registered in your name. I'll get you the forms off the internet. We fill them out and send them in and it's done. Nothing she can do to stop you. You're the father, you have rights, too!"

"Yeah, Son. Rights!" Dad was onto his third beer while I still had my second at my lips. "Don't let that bitch control you with the kid. Your mother tried that on me. I never told you this, but she did. Women use kids like weapons." This got a nasty look from Marg but she said nothing. "You need to do what Marg says. Take charge. Be a man. Register the kid in your name and then YOU decide if you're gonna let her come home."

"Which is how come our daughter was registered as Laura Olivier Lethbridge. LOL. Laugh Out Loud. Get it? Sarah was pissed but by the time she found out, it was too friggin' late!

Part Five – Sarah

Baby Blues

I cried myself to sleep every night. Strapped to the bed, up to my eyeballs in sedatives and who knew what. I was a wreck, physically and emotionally, and I really don't think being in a looney bin was doing me any good. Well, I think that now but I can think now, I couldn't think straight for two seconds back then. I was upset all the time, cried at anything and just wanted to be by myself. It all began about three weeks after Laura was born. I made the mistake of moving back with Stewart. It was his idea.

"Look, you belong in your own home, not here with your mum and dad. With me. And Laura."

"I dunno, Stewart. I just…"

"You gotta come back. We're a family now. I need you, sweets."

That did it, I think. Him calling me 'sweets' again. First time in months. First time since I told him I was pregnant. I wanted us to be a family, doesn't every mother? I forgot all the horrible things that had happened between us and just wanted to start again. Start fresh.

"Let's tell your mum and dad when they come back, but meanwhile, we'll pack your things and take you home, OK?"

I just nodded and sat there on the bed holding Laura while Stewart packed my bags and put them in the car. Then he came back and grabbed the baby things. When we got to the Commodore he strapped the baby capsule in the back and I sat next to it, looking at Laura sleeping, just her little face poking out of the blanket. We drove back to our flat and it felt strange walking in. The place had been tidied up, probably Marg or Mary because I know there was no way Stewart would have bothered.

"The place looks nice, Stewart."

"Yeah, er, I did some housekeeping before I come over. Make it nice for you and Laura."

"Thanks, love. I appreciate that."

"Put Laura down and sit here on the bed with me."

I did as he asked and as soon as I sat next to him he was all over me. I felt a bit panicky, I don't know why but I just didn't feel like getting intimate. "Not yet, love. Please, give me some time, OK?"

"What? It's been months. C'mon. You can't say no, we're a family. You're my woman. I need…"

And so he did it. He used me, I just lay there. I didn't want to but, I dunno. I just had no interest in sex. I didn't want to say no because it would make him angry and I just couldn't cope with that. To be honest, I could barely cope with Laura. Sometimes she'd cry and I just couldn't get up and see to her. I wanted to talk to my mum but her and Dad had gone to Hawaii for a holiday. They took Billy with them. I wish they'd taken me, too. If they had, none of what went on after I moved back to the flat would have happened.

What 'happened' began when Mary and Marg came by. 'Just dropped in' they said. More like an ambush.

"So, Sarah. Stewart tells me you are not coping."

That was Mary. Damn Stewart! Why couldn't he keep his mouth shut? Running off and telling his mum and Marg our private business.

"I understand. It's tough being a mum for the first time. I remember with…" and off she went. Marg kept throwing her two cents in. By the time they had finished their coffee I was a wreck. Mary said I had 'post partum depression' but if it was really serious, maybe 'post partum psychosis'. I was scared.

"Psychosis? Isn't that like being mentally ill or something?"

"Sweetie, there's no shame in being mentally ill these days. The brain is just another organ. It can get sick like your heart or your kidneys."

"Yes, but people on dialysis don't get locked away in straight jackets."

"Oh don't be silly, Sarah. Nobody gets locked away in straight jackets these days." This was Marg, throwing in another two cents worth. "Look, you just have a heavy dose of the 'Baby Blues'. That's what they called it in my day. These days they use fancy words and make it sound worse than it is. You just need a rest."

"Marg's right, Sarah. Where I work, well it's more like a resort than a hospital, at least the residential wing for mental patients is."

"Mental patient. It sounds so… I dunno, so bad. Like I'm a serial killer or something. I'm not ill, I'm just, well, I just find it hard to cope, that's all."

"Sarah, the thing that manages coping is your brain. If that is not working a hundred percent, and it happens to everyone to some degree at some stage in their lives, then that is a mental illness. Nothing to be ashamed about."

I wasn't feeling ashamed, at least not up to that moment, but the more they fired at me, soothing, reassuring, the more I felt there was something wrong with me and the more I did feel ashamed. I felt like I wanted to run away and hide.

"Sarah, you have all the classic signs and symptoms. You have no interest in sex, you don't eat, you can't sleep, you feel exhausted, empty, overwhelmed. You aren't coping except by avoiding what has to be done. Trust me, sweetie. I'm a nurse. I have seen this before more times than I care to remember. You are suffering post partum depression. It happens to twenty five percent of mothers. Hell, it even happens to twenty five percent of fathers!"

She was right, I found out later. It does happen to a lot of parents, maybe not that many but a lot and it is still not fully researched or understood. I know that now but back then I couldn't even google the term. They kept this up for two hours and four cups of coffee and in the end I just gave in. They took me to Mary's doctor and he referred me to a specialist at the private hospital Mary worked at and by ten the next morning I was in my nightie in a room with another young mum. We barely said two words to each other, both of us just wanted to crawl under the covers and ignore the world. I had top health cover and so I didn't worry about what this was all costing. Marg said she'd make sure Stewart told my parents and not to worry about anything. She and Mary would care for Laura and all I had to do was rest and get better. But I got worse.

"I think we need to adjust your medication, Sarah." That was the doctor. I didn't even know his name. He had a name tag and an ID badge and he had told me but I just wasn't taking anything in. I was on some powerful sedatives and I didn't care about anything. It was like I was tripping on drugs, I suppose. Which in a way I was but not street drugs like heroin or meth. These were prescription drugs. Medication. I never saw Mary except on the first day. She dropped off some of my things and said she would come back but she didn't. Worked another ward, I think. Marg came with Stewart the next day, stayed for half an hour then left me to myself. I was glad at the time but then I never saw any of them again. The whole month they kept me there.

I must have had a reaction to the new medication because I ended up strapped to the bed. I felt like a prisoner and I guess I was. I screamed out for my mum and dad and for Stewart and Laura and nobody heard me. Nobody came. I just withdrew into myself and cried. They changed the medication again and then they stopped it altogether and all I wanted to do was go home. I told the doctors and the nurses. Every morning four or five of them would traipse into my room. Students. Then the doctor would start talking about me as if I wasn't there, telling them of my symptoms and treatment. I couldn't take any of it in. Just lay there on my side, facing away from them and staring at the window. The blinds were always drawn and I had no idea what was beyond them. I think it was the worst time of my life and if I wasn't depressed when I went in, I was certainly depressed by the time they thought I was cured.

I lost all track of time, didn't even remember what day it was unless I asked a nurse. I looked at my chart one morning and counted the days. Twenty nine days. On the thirtieth day, my mum and dad came to see me. To take me home. Rescue me. I cried even more.

"We didn't know, love." Mum was crying almost as much as I was.

"If we'd known where you were, Sarah, I mean. Look, there's no way we'd have let this happen to you." Dad was almost blubbing too.

"Marg said Stewart called you. She said he'd let you know where I was so you could visit me but you never came." I was sitting on the sofa, wrapped in a blanket and letting Mum hug me like I was four years old again. Dad had the giant size box of tissues on the coffee able and I was doing a good job of depleting the world's paper production.

"Stewart did call, but not until yesterday. I went off! Asked him why did he wait a month. We would have flown straight back from Hawaii if we'd known." Dad was very upset. Angry, frustrated, he'd said he felt ashamed he'd not been there for me but I didn't blame him. How could he be there if he didn't know where 'there' was? He didn't even know there was a 'there'! No, the fault lay with Stewart. He knew I was there. Or Marg. She helped put me there. Or Mary for suggesting it. She did seem like she genuinely felt it was the best thing for me but I realised Marg and Stewart had done it for other reasons. They had an agenda, as they say. I just couldn't for the life of me figure out what it could be at that time. It wouldn't be long before I found out.

***

"You can't see her."

"He actually said that?"

"That's all he said. Then he hung up on me!" I burst into tears again. Seemed like all I was doing was crying. Getting kicked in the guts and crying.

"He actually said; 'you can't see her', yeah?" Mum was shocked and couldn't believe Stewart had said that to me. I'd called him on his mobile and said I was out of hospital and where was Laura?

"She's with me."

That was it. Nothing more, just that. I asked him was she at home, at the flat and he just laughed. It was more of a snicker than a laugh, evil like.

"You can have your crappy flat back. Tell your dad to shove it up his arse. I've got me own place now. Me and Laura. And Emma."

I couldn't believe it! He'd moved out of our flat and in with some tart. I thought I knew which Emma he was referring to, a fat mole who hung out down the pub and slept with anyone who bought her a drink or some drugs. She took anything from marijuana to Rohipnol and who knew what she was doing with my daughter. It wouldn't be taking proper care of him and there was no way Stewart would have suddenly become the doting single parent father type.

"Emma? That fat slut from the pub?"

"Watch your mouth, slag!"

"Don't you…" I was going to hit back but I realised that would just piss him off more. As Dad says, you catch more flies with honey than vinegar. I had to suck it up for Laura's sake. "Stewart, please. I want to see my baby. My daughter. Our daughter. Please!" I almost said 'I'm begging you' but I caught myself in time. If I got that low so soon I'd have nothing left to say.

"No way! You're not a fit mother, are ya?"

I was stunned. I couldn't believe what he just said.

"What do you mean? Of course I'm a fit… How dare you say that."

"No, you're not a fit mother and you aren't going to hurt my kid."

"He's our kid! Our daughter! I'm her mother! I gave birth to her! You never even wanted her…"

"Well somebody has to care for the little bugger and it's obvious you're not fit. That's official!"

"What? What do you mean, 'official'? I don't understand?" I was starting to panic. I'd perked up two hundred percent since Mum and Dad got me out of that hospital. They weren't going to release me since it wasn't Mum or Dad that signed me in. They tried to make out only the person who signed me in could sign me out and that would have been Marg. Dad was having none of it and nearly dragged the ward sister over the desk. Instead he leaned across, really close and almost whispered that if she didn't start the release process he would be back with a Writ of Habeas Corpus and half a dozen coppers. I doubt she knew what Habeas Corpus meant but she produced my body in ten minutes, dressed, packed and ready to go.

"I said, it's official. You are not a fit person to have custody of a baby. You are a nutter, remember?"

"I am not a nutter! I was suffering PPD. Post-partum Depression, it is a common…"

"Not in my family it's not. No nutters in the Lethbridge family. Your lot are the mental cases and no mental case is looking after my daughter."

"I'm not mental! You bastard!" I lost it then. I went off. I told him he was evil, nasty, mean and a lot of other things and it was a minute or two before I realised I was talking to thin air. He'd hung up. I just sat there. Slid down the wall and crumpled into a ball on the floor, still holding my mobile and sobbing. That was how Mum found me.

"We'll find her, love. Your dad will. He won't let him get away with this. Laura's our grandchild, too. We have rights, as grandparents. We'll find her and bring her home. There, there, love. C'mon, dry your eyes."

Good old Mum. Always there when you needed her and if she didn't know what to do, she knew Dad would find a solution. He always did, but this time... This time I wasn't sure. This time I felt like my world was ended, over with, finished. Or maybe that was what I should do? Finish it? That was the first time, there in the kitchen, still holding my mobile phone, I actually thought the word 'suicide'. It seemed so clear, so logical. The perfect solution. The only solution. If Mum hadn't been there to hold me and love me, I dunno. I just don't.

Challenger Deep

If I thought I had reached rock bottom when I was in the hospital, it was nothing to how low I sunk after that phone call to Stewart. I was now at the bottom of the ocean. There was no direction to go in other than sideways or up. The deepest point in the ocean is a place called the Challenger Deep. It is 10.911 km below the surface. The pressure at that point is 1086 bars, meaning over 1,000 times the pressure you feel at sea level. And it is cold, maybe 1 degree Celsius. I know this because I looked it up on Wikipedia. Until then I didn't know where I was but now I knew. I was at Challenger Deep. I couldn't sink any lower and it was cold and lonely. The pressure I was feeling was a thousand times more than anything I had ever felt in my life and I was tearing myself apart every day I couldn't see my baby. I told Dad about how I felt and what I'd read on Wikipedia, about being in the deepest part of the ocean.

"Well, look on the bright side, petal."

"There's a bright side, Dad?"

"Yes. There is."

"Sorry. I can't see it."

"That's because it's bloody dark down where you are, Sarah. And you know what you do when it is dark, don't you?"

"What?"

"You turn on the bleeding lights, my sweet! Turn on the bleeding lights!"

I didn't get it. What the hell was Dad waffling on about? Lights? There wasn't any light in my life right then. "The only light in my life, Dad, is Laura and she's not here. Shit! I don't even know where she is! Or how to find her."

"Well I do. There are only two places she could be. Think, Sarah. You know Stewart better than I do. Where would he go if he has a baby to look after. A two and a half month old baby. It is pretty demanding, right?"

"Yes. She needs feeding…"

"And changing and burping. I know, we're doing it with Billy. Same age, remember?"

"How could I not?" Which nearly had me bawling again but I was getting better; getting tougher. I still cried a lot but not constantly like before. 'What doesn't kill you makes you stronger' as Dad was fond of reminding me. I had thought about killing myself a couple of times since that first time on the kitchen floor but something kept me going. Kept putting it off. I realise now I was not ready and I knew, somehow, despite how messed up my mind was; it wasn't the answer. It's never the answer. Funny how it seemed so absolutely, logically, perfectly correct at the time, though. But then if your head's not on straight these ideas do seem sensible. The old, 'seemed like a good idea at the time' thing. "I have to stay alive, Dad. For Laura."

"And for your mum and me, Sarah. And for yourself. We didn't bring you into this world to stand idly by and watch you destroy yourself because of some piece of amoeba like Stewart."

"Piece of amoeba?"

"You know what I mean. Microscopic crap and all that."

We laughed and I felt better, the best I'd felt for a long time. Dad was always able to make me laugh and the Reader's Digest are right; laughter is the best medicine.

"So, pet. Where? Where would Stewart go? He needs help to care for the baby. He needs it to be cheap, if not free, because he is on the compo and no doubt he needs domestic arrangements. Unless he learned how to do his own laundry all of a sudden."

"His mum's or Marg. Who else could it be?"

"Emma. Or her mum's place."

"That Emma isn't the type to have her own place. She bludges off other people and I doubt she knew her mother."

"Whatever you do, Sarah, don't ever underestimate your opponent and try to have some compassion for her. She might have very valid reasons she ended up like this and let's not be the ones to judge, OK? Especially not when we don't really know her."

"Yeah, I guess so. Who knows why she cracks on to any bloke she can, especially other chick's guys. I doubt she is even living with him, to be honest."

"What makes you say that?"

"Nothing in it for her other than having to play mum to some other woman's kid. She's just out for a good time. Booze, drugs and what have you, and she pays for it with her body. Doesn't fit the profile, as they say on those CSI shows."

Now it was Dad's turn to laugh. "Jeez, Sarah, sometimes you just surprise me and sometimes you amaze me. That's pretty clever. I think you are spot on. He probably just threw in that bit about living with Emma to make you jealous. So if we cross her off the list who are we left with? Mary or Marg, right?"

"Right. Well Mary is the grandmother, so maybe..."

"But she lives miles away and Stewart relies too much on his social network, such as it is, around here. I doubt he'd leave that for long."

"True, he needs his mates and his pub and he's too lazy to find out where everything is in a new place. I think you're right. Not Mary's. So…"

"So it must be Marg's."

"Makes sense, Dad."

"Just one problem. A minor detail but a problem all the same."

"Oh? What's that."

"Well she has moved, as you know." I did know. Marg had told me she and Nathan were moving into a cheaper place after Dad gave her notice. Actually he gave her ten minutes notice but a month's pay in lieu. He didn't have to as she was paid weekly but he said she'd been a good employee for years before going off the rails lately and he didn't want any hassle with the unfair dismissal laws. She made out she didn't hold it against me at all, which I sarcastically said that was big of her. She'd ignored my remark and went on to say they'd be moving out of their current place but wouldn't be going far. 'Had too much to do in the area' she had said, but didn't elaborate. Either way I didn't pay much attention. This was just before she had me admitted to the hospital; or was that committed? She must have moved house right after they locked me up. Coincidence?

"Didn't she leave a forwarding address at the factory, Dad?"

"Nope. Said she'd let me know before tax time so I knew where to send her group certificate, but you can send them by email nowadays so maybe she was never going to tell me. Anyway, I'm sure wherever she and Nathan are, Stewart and Laura are there too."

"Well, we'll check out her Facebook page, unless she's blocked us. We have mutual friends so if she posts on one of those we might be able to see it if it is shared. I dunno, however that social media works, we'll find her."

"I doubt she'd bother to change her address on the electoral roll and I'll check the telephone directory but she probably just has a mobile, no landline. Never mind, we'll find her. She has to surface some time. Maybe Nathan will tell his mates down the pub and one of them lets it slip. You never know."

***

The next two weeks I tried to get myself back to normal. I went back to work and took over Marg's job. Dad had me sort through all the accounts while he got back into marketing. Business had died off the past few months but he soon had orders coming in every day and it picked up in no time. He was good like that, once he set his mind to something, he just went and did it. The boys were happy again. More and more 'Marg' stories came out. Seemed she wasn't liked very much by the workers but none of them wanted to risk her wrath by telling Dad or Mum. I also found so many paid bills that just didn't match the rest of the paperwork for dozens of jobs.

"Here's another one, Dad. Five hundred and thirty dollars for 'fixtures', billed to the Clansman Consulting job. But there's nothing fitting that amount on the materials list, the quote, the sign off sheet, nothing."

"Jeez! Look at this! Two friggin' grand for 'site preparation'. What bloody site preparation? Who did it? 'Jagson Holdings Pty Ltd?' Never heard of them."

"Jagson Holdings? Hang on, I found one before from them. Over three thousand, hold on, here!" I produced the invoice, marked paid in full, from a company claiming to have done work for us on one of our big corporate jobs. That job was over a hundred grand and there were nearly fifty different invoices for various sub-contractors and materials, no wonder this one slid under the radar."

"When's it for? What date?"

I looked at the date and it was months ago, back when Dad and Mum were overseas getting the IVF. I checked the other dodgy invoices and they were all for the same period, or some other time when Dad and Mum were out of the country and Marg was left to look after the business.

"Well she certainly looked after her business! That bitch! She stole from me. From us, the family. We trusted her. I trusted her!"

Dad was really upset. The stolen money hurt, but I know him. What hurt far more was the breach of his trust.

"I can't believe this. Look, here's one going back three years, you know, when I took your mum to Kenya to see the lions. We're going to have to go through all the paperwork from when she started, count up just how much she took us for."

"It's not just fake invoices for work never done or materials never delivered. Look at this one." I showed him an invoice that was made out to Roger Green and Sons, a genuine company we had worked for since the day Dad opened the doors. "This invoice is for five grand. This invoice," I held up another one with the same invoice number printed on it, "is for nearly six grand. The invoice for the larger amount was down the back of the filing cabinet."

"What? I don't understand. Same invoice number. Same date, same details, same everything but different amounts?"

"Yeah, how can you have the same invoice number? They are printed consecutively with three copies, four pages in total, all with the same number. Then the next page is the next number in the sequence. So how…?"

"Two sets of invoice books. Identical numbers."

"But how? How'd she get two invoice books with the same numbers?"

"Sarah. Think. Who organizes the stationery? Who gets the invoice books and order books printed?"

"That bitch!"

"That bitch is right. That very clever, cunning bitch. We need to find the second book, or books. I bet she took them with her. Probably keeps them at home. Shit!"

"What now?"

"Remember when she was off sick and it was end of year and she offered to work from home to catch up on the paperwork? She said she was telecommuting."

"Yes, she'd do the data entry stuff from her laptop… oh dear." It had just dawned on me what Dad had just realised. We were screwed. Marg was given access to the company computer via the internet so she could work at home. She said she was quarantined for the flu or some virus but was well enough to work. She made a big deal about knowing it was costing us money to pay her sick leave but not get any work out of her so she wanted to work from home. Dad thought she was wonderful for being so loyal and hardworking.

"I bet she tapped into the system and copied everything. Then she would update things at night after work from her laptop. Clean up the loose ends. She had the spare invoice and order books at home, too. She'd send the customer the one for the big amount, they'd pay and she'd move the money around from home before putting the copy of the invoice with the lower amount into the file. Bring up the bank account, Sarah. Let's check some of these dates and amounts against the invoices."

I accessed our online banking and started with the fake invoice I'd found down the back of the cabinet. I couldn't believe it!

"Look Dad. See the date on the invoice? Well here is the deposit into the account for the lower amount. I dunno, why would Roger Greens pay the lesser amount if she sent them the fake invoice for a grand more?"

"Maybe she didn't send that one, changed her mind?"

"No the invoice we have is one of the copies, not the original the client gets."

"Call 'em up. Ask Fatima in accounts to track that invoice and their payment."

I called the accounts manager at Roger Green and Sons, we did so much work for them I had Fatima's number on speed dial. She was curious as to why we were chasing such an old invoice. I didn't want to say too much so I just said I was going back over old invoices for a tax audit. She came back in a minute or two and gave me the details. I said thanks, hung up and turned to look at Dad. I was still trying to figure out what this all meant.

"Well?"

"Huh?"

"What'd she say? Fatima? What did she say?"

Their invoice is for the six grand. She says they paid it on 30 days, same as always. She's emailing me a scan of the deposit details. She says it was paid the same as every other invoice we have sent them for the last two years since we changed our bank."

"What? Changed our... We've been with Mike at the NAB since we landed in the country!"

I knew that. Uncle Mike, as I called our bank manager, had worked with Dad back in the UK. He'd migrated the year before us and when we arrived he was already working at the local branch and it seemed sensible to open an account with him. In fact, I remember Dad telling us Mike opened the account for us before we migrated so we had it operating with money already in the account when we arrived. The only other account we had there apart from the business one was Mum and Dad's private account. And mine, of course. I had been banking with them since I got my first pay working in the business after school and on weekends.

"Look, here's the email. Here's the account number they pay us through. Here's our account. Different number. Even the BSB's not the same. Same bank, different branch."

"The thieving cow! How friggin' big is this?" Dad was stunned and so was I. Marg had not only had fake invoice and order books printed, she had opened a bank account in the company name and had all the payments deposited into it. Then she transferred most of those payments to our genuine business account while keeping the balance.

"How much?"

"Dad?"

"How much has she cost us?"

"I dunno, a lot."

"Sarah. I'm not talking just the money. I'm talking business. We quote on jobs and it is accepted, then she over charges and no doubt rings them up and gives them some bullshit excuse and they pay the larger amount. I mean it isn't much in the grand scheme of things compared to what they are paying all up, but it adds up. It might also piss them off and next time we tender for a job we get knocked back because they remember how the last few jobs we always went over the quote."

"Wouldn't they ring and say something to you?"

"Yeah, if they wanted to keep us on but probably they just use someone else. Say nothing. Customers who complain are doing you a favour. At least you know there may be a problem you have to fix. Most customers who have a problem just say nothing and never come back. Hey tell everyone they know about how you gave them bad service, just don't bother to tell us so we can do something about it. No wonder!"

"No wonder what, Dad?"

No bloody wonder repeat business has been dropping off. You can only bill the customer for more than the quote so many times and they just go somewhere else. That's why business has been down, Sarah. We stopped looking for new clients, thinking we were doing great work for existing ones. We were, we do, but if we've been hitting them for 'cost over runs'... No bloody wonder!"

"That bitch!"

"That thieving, lying cow!"

The Plot Thickens

"Sarah. We got her!" Dad was almost yelling down his mobile.

"Where? Where is she? How'd you find her?"

"The police called and said they were taking her in for questioning over my complaint about her embezzling all that money. They knew where to find her but of course, they weren't saying where she lives. So I just said, 'oh, I was coming in to see you but I don't want to risk running into her. When will she be there?'. They said she was already there and they expected to charge her but she would be bailed, probably let go before tea time. So I…"

"So that's where you've been! Mum was wondering but didn't want to ask. You've been staking out the cop shop waiting for her to be released, right?"

"Yeah, then when she came out, I thought she'd be in there for weeks I waited so long, but when she come out she got a cab and I followed her home."

"Cab? Why didn't Nathan, or even Stewart pick her up?"

"No idea, probably did a runner for the border when the cops knocked on the door and started searching the place. Anyway, I know where she lives now so next thing, I wait here until Stewart shows up and we can confirm the baby is here too."

"Then what, Dad?" In all the excitement it finally dawned on me that just knowing where Laura was wasn't enough. We needed to have a plan for what we'd do after that. "How am I going to get my Laura back?"

"I dunno, love. I'll think of something. I reckon we can just go in and take her back. You are her mother, afterall. I think so long as you are the one to lay hands upon her and take her off the premises, he hasn't got a leg to stand on."

That sounded good, but I couldn't help feeling there was something missing. Something we hadn't picked up on that would make whatever we did doomed to failure. "I dunno, Dad, that sounds great on the telly but this is my life, not a tv show. What if he doesn't open the door? You can't just kick it in like on the movies. You'll get arrested and then where will we be?" Well with Mum not here at the moment, someone had to think sensibly!

"You sound just like your mother. Look, first things first, ok? We gotta find the baby before we can do anything. That means we need to sight her and get an idea of her routine. We need to know her movements and those of Stewart and whoever else before we can risk a snatch-op."

"Snatch-op? You're beginning to sound like one of those military briefers they put up in front of the media microphones to tell you how well the war's going for our side."

"Well possession is nine tenths of the law! If we have Laura then Stewart is the one that has to ask you for visitation."

"I don't want to make Laura a weapon against Stewart." That was the last thing I wanted for Stewart, for Laura, for me. Nobody wins custody battles. "I just want my baby so I can be a mother to her. A proper mother."

"I know, pet but face the facts. Stewart is doing precisely that. Using Laura as a weapon against you. A weapon to control you, to hurt you. I don't know why or what drove him to turn like he has, but he has and he's doing it."

"Dad!"

"Whether you like it or not, Sarah. Stewart is using Laura to hurt you and that hurts me and your mother." Dad was right. Stewart was hurting me. Part of me still loved him, no matter what he'd said and done. He was the father of our baby but, well, he was denying me any access. All I had was his mobile phone number and he wasn't answering my calls and rarely returning my text messages. When he did they were one word yes or no answers or snide, sarcastic remarks. Usually about me being a looney. Nobody asks to suffer postpartum depression, it chooses you, not the other way around. Yet once you have the stigma of having suffered a mental illness, no matter how minor, no matter if you are cured you are never treated the same way again. I don't care what anyone says, it's true. Once someone knows you had a mental illness they look at you differently, even those who love you the most. I know Mum and Dad had changed. Not in a big way, but in little ways. The way they seemed to be over concerned about some things and always asking me twice, as if to reassure themselves I was normal again.

"So what are you saying, Dad? I mean, what do we do next?"

"Hire a hit man and have him rubbed out."

"Dad!"

"I'm joking, love. Although I confess the thought has crossed my mind once or twice. It's just the frustration of being so bloody powerless. They have the baby, they hold all the cards. Stewart has as much right to custody of the child as you do. The courts…"

"Courts? When did this go to court?"

"Face facts, Sarah, it will, sooner or later. What alternative do we have? Ask him nicely to bring Laura back? You tried that a million times already."

"Yes, but court. I mean, how much would that cost. A thousand dollars?"

"And the rest. Try tens of thousands, even hundreds of thousands. Once you sign on to pay a solicitor's son's school fees for the next five years it gets expensive. Or you pay off their investment property. The only people who win court cases are the lawyers."

"Well there's no way Stewart can afford that."

"He won't have to. We would bring the case against him and if we win he doesn't have to pay because I doubt they would level costs against an unemployed bloke who has to somehow find the money to pay child support. If he wins, we will have to pay his costs."

"That's not fair!"

"Fair? Fair? Sarah, nothing in this life is fair unless you make it fair. The system is not set up to be fair but to make as much money for the lawyers as possible. Why do you think nearly everyone in parliament used to be a lawyer? They figured out the best place to make money out of law was to make the law."

I knew where this was heading. Dad would go on about how the rich were exploiting the rest of us, owning politicians and making laws to suit themselves while hard working small businesses and wage earners did all the heavy lifting with taxes. I'm sure he was spot on but I didn't want to hear it right then.

"Dad, I don't want to go to court. I can't afford to win let alone lose. We have to find another way. I just want my baby back." Which was when I lost it. I just started crying and couldn't stop. Dad tried to comfort me but nothing he could say was getting through. I was slipping back into depression.

"Sarah, we'll find a way. Look on the bright side, at least we know where he might be. I'll wait here a while and see if he shows up. You make yourself a cuppa and try and stay positive, alright?"

"Yeah, thanks Dad." I hung up and did as he said. Made a cup of coffee and sat on the lounge. The coffee went cold while I just sat there and cried. In the end I stuck it in the microwave to heat it up, nearly burnt the roof of my mouth when it was done and threw the lot down the sink. Then I cried some more.

***

Dad watched Marg's place for two days. He saw nobody but Nathan or Marg, and then only rarely. I think he'd had enough and didn't bother going on the third day. I kept sending text messages to Stewart but the only reply was the one where he said if I keep harassing him he'll report me for stalking. He went on to say he had kept a record of my fifty three text messages in a week and that they were 'evidence'. Evidence of what? His refusal to give me the courtesy of a reply? Then he changed tactics and it was me who starting keeping a record of his texts. He began to answer my messages with nasty replies, always alluding to how I was an unfit mother, a looney, and how I should be locked up and not let near any children and especially not Laura.

'you are not fit to be a mum Laura is much better now shez with me'

'stop txtg me u r a ntcse'

I think 'ntcse' meant nutcase. He used to write 'looney' as 'luny', probably too lazy to spell it out, if he could spell. I would try and keep it calm and controlled and not lose my rag but sometimes he drove me up the wall. He knew how to push all of my buttons and basically he just played with me. Played with my mind, my emotions, my need for Laura. The more he twisted things around the more I began to lose it again.

'u r not fit to be lauras mum. No way will she have a luny for a mother.'

These texts came in all day and all night for a week. I had over a hundred of them on my phone but I didn't want to report him because any contact was better than no contact. I knew too well what it was like to be left alone, completely alone with no contact or communication with anyone. They'd done it to me in the hospital for hours and hours, waiting till I was asleep to deliver my meals so they would be cold when I woke up. I told the nurses and the doctors and they said I was imagining things, part of the PPD. I told Dad later and he swore they don't do things like that in hospitals in Australia, but they did. I know they did. I didn't want to be ignored ever again so I didn't report the texts. I didn't even tell Dad or Mum because I knew they would just tell me to switch off my phone or not read the messages. Easy for them, they had their Billy. They had each other. I felt like I didn't even have them some times.

Life just seemed to drag on, going nowhere. Half the time I couldn't get myself out of bed to go to work, so I didn't. I just stayed in bed all day. I couldn't be bothered eating and I lost weight. My baby tummy disappeared and I could fit clothes I wore before I was pregnant again. At the rate I was going, though, it wouldn't have been long before they would have been hanging off me.

"Sarah, you got to get a grip, love."

This was Mum talking, giving me the 'get a grip' lecture. It was her favourite phrase. Get a grip. Get a grip on yourself. Well I gripped my arms across my chest and just stood there, not really listening, just making the odd mouth noise when it seemed appropriate. I'd heard it all before when I was a teenager and I had that run in with anorexia. Not for long but long enough to get pretty skinny. Skinny enough to be noticed, which was why I was not eating back then. But not noticed by Mum. She did notice and she went off. She found my school lunches still in my bag, uneaten, or hidden in my wardrobe. I couldn't bring myself to put them in the garbage bin at school. Apart from worrying if anyone saw me I just couldn't waste food like that. I had been brought up with the old 'millions starving in Africa' line and 'when we were kids we had nothing to eat but bread and dripping'. Which was a lie. Maybe Gran and Granddad had that during the Blitz or whatever it was they went through but Mum and Dad grew up in the 1960s and 70s and while they may have done it tough, they never went hungry. Funny how parents exaggerate like that. I'll probably say the same shit to Laura one day.

"I've got a grip, Mum."

"Grip? You haven't! You haven't been out of the house for three days, out of bed for two. This is the first time we've seen you upright and vertical for a week!"

"Upright and vertical are the same thing, Mum."

"You know what I mean, don't change the subject. No, Sarah, we're worried sick about you. You are not improving, in fact, you're getting worse. You have to pull yourself together, love!"

"Together? How can I be together when I don't have my baby?'

"Don't be…"

"What? Don't be what, Mum? Don't be stupid? Don't be selfish? Don't be such a loser? Don't be such a waste of space, an oxygen thief? Which is it?" I'd lost it. I was lashing out at Mum because she was there and Stewart wasn't.

"Sarah! Get a grip of yourself!"

"Grip your bloody self, Mum!"

"SARAH! Don't you talk to your mother like that! Not under this roof!" Dad was wading in now. He'd been in the lounge and probably heard me going off. "Your mother and I are just concerned for you. Deeply concerned. And for Billy."

"Bill… Billy? I wouldn't hurt Billy!"

"Adam!" Mum gave Dad the look she keeps in reserve for when she is mightily pissed off at Dad and is letting him know he has screwed up. I figured they had been talking among themselves and somehow figured I might be dangerous to their baby boy. I was shocked, no, I was more than that. I was deeply hurt.

"Dad! I would never do anything to hurt Billy. Or you or Mum. Never!"

"I didn't mean that, Sarah. I meant, well, I know, we know, your mum and I, we know you wouldn't do anything on purpose but…"

"But what?"

"Sarah, your dad doesn't mean…"

"What? What doesn't he mean?"

"Love. C'mon, you have to be reasonable. I mean…"

"You mean I'm a looney, a nutcase, just like Stewart keeps saying every time he texts me."

"No, I mean… what? Stewart is texting you?" Dad looked at Mum, then back at me.

"Stewart has been texting you?" Mum sounded like Dad's echo.

"Yes. Calling me a looney and a nutcase and an unfit mother and now you're saying you think I'll harm Billy."

"We said nothing of the sort!" Dad was getting pretty wound up. I could tell by the way he was going red in the cheeks and the way he kept clenching his fists and his teeth, keeping himself under control. I do the same thing.

"Yes you did! You just did! You said you were concerned for me and Billy. I would never…"

"That's not what I said. You're twisting my words. I'm, we're," he said, pointing at Mum, "we're concerned about you full stop, new sentence. We are concerned about how this might be affecting Billy. Full stop. New paragraph we are concerned about how it is affecting us."

"Sarah, love. We've had nothing but drama in our lives for months now. A year or more. Not our drama. Your drama. We can't cope. We've got our own problems to deal with and we love you dearly, we will always love you, but…"

"But we need some space, pet. We need to have some space, some time with Billy."

"What do you mean? Space?" I could hardly breathe. My heart was pounding in my ears and I felt like the world was shrinking, closing in on me, tighter and tighter.

"Your dad got you a new flat, love. Not far away, nicer. He furnished it nice, too."

"Yeah, I got your stuff moved in, what he left behind of it. Bastard stole half your things. Things me and your mum bought and paid for."

"Adam! Sarah, it's for the best. For all of us. You need your independence too, love. We need ours. I'm sorry."

"You're abandoning me then?" I was devastated. Now I had no one. No Laura, no Stewart, no Mum, no Dad. Nobody!

"No love. We're not abandoning you. We love you. We'll always be here for you. It's just we need some space. This is all too hard for us. It's not our fight but we'll fight it with you." Mum was crying too, now.

"But we need to fight it on separate battlefields, you know. We need to…"

"I know. You need your space." And that was that.

Home Alone

Just like the movie, I was home alone. It was a lovely flat; great view of the ocean and a huge balcony big enough for a table, chairs, BBQ, pot plants and still space left over for dancing. It was the ideal party flat; except I had no friends to party with and even had I hundreds, I just felt like jumping over the balcony rail. Actually it was called a 'balustrade'. The real estate agent had snootily corrected Dad when she was showing us through the place. Balcony rail, balustrade, whatever you called it, the thing was mostly glass with a stainless steel rail along the top wide enough to put your drinks and nibblies on and just high enough you couldn't sit on it without your feet leaving the floor. I liked the glass fence panels, even sitting on the banana lounge beside the outdoor dining setting you could gaze out over the ocean. I liked the balcony full stop. I just didn't like being abandoned here by my parents.

"It is a full security building, pet." Dad was telling me all the 'plusses', selling me the 'sizzle' as Mum often said.

"Your dad could sell the frost off a glass of icy cold beer." Mum had a slew of them; 'snow to eskimoes', 'sand to the arabs' and 'shower curtains to vegetarians'. I have absolutely no idea what that last one means but they always thought it was funny.

"See, there's an intercom. Nobody can get in without you letting them in. Even if someone else lets them into the building, they have to get past the CCTV in the corridor, plus the peep hole. No way they can get into your flat without you opening the door and you only open it to people you sight and want to let in."

"I can't think who that will be."

"Aww, c'mon, Sarah! We've been over this. We need to take a break."

"I wish I could take a break from my life."

"Well, be reasonable, pet, that's not our…"

"Adam, no. Sarah, we need to get away for a while. We need our own family time. With Billy."

"So I'm not family anymore? Is that what you're saying?" I know I was being unreasonable but this was how I felt and I felt abandoned, alone, exiled, unloved. It was horrible.

"Sarah." Dad used his 'please be reasonable' tone. I'd heard it so many times, I knew what was coming next so I turned away and mouthed the words as he spoke them. "Please, be reasonable."

"Sarah! Don't mock your father! Be serious!" Mum must have seen me, probably reflected in the full length hall mirror.

"So what's it going to be? Reasonable or serious?"

"Don't be a smart arse, Sarah."

"What if I'm a reasonable smart arse, Dad?"

""Oh, good grief. Grow up Sarah. C'mon Adam, we have better things to be doing." Mum grabbed her bag and headed for the front door. Dad gave me a look, a squeeze on the shoulders and he followed Mum to the door. At the door Mum turned, gave me a peck on the cheek and said; "Get it together, love. For your sake, for our sakes, for the baby's sake."

"Take care, love. We will be online every day, or you can call us if you need anything. You got money in the bank to live on. Just look after the business, OK? Kris is good but still learning, so be there for her, yeah?" Kris was the new office manager Dad had hired to replace Marg. As Dad said, she was experienced but still learning her way around our office. I would be in every day to help and keep an eye on things. At least that was the plan.

I closed the door behind them and did that movie thing people do at door closing time. You know, where you spin around, lean back against the door and then just slide down it to the floor? I did that and just sat there, legs crossed, head back against the solid wood of the door, doing nothing, thinking nothing, feeling everything. I must have sat there for ten minutes before the cold tiles soaked through my shorts and numbed my bum enough to motivate me to move. I went out on the balcony, it was a short dogleg like walk from entry vestibule (another of the real estate agent's terms) across the main reception room (I think she was trying to impress Dad, she knew what the Poms called a living room) and past the open kitchen-dining area to the french doors leading onto the balcony. The balcony ran the full length of the flat and around the corner with a second sliding door into the bedroom. I could run laps. The bedroom was big and airy and had an ensuite bathroom and a walk-in wardrobe that was bigger than my old bedroom at home. Home. This is my home now. Home for me was always where my parents were but no longer. They'd made that very clear. It was time to leave the nest once and for all. Stand on my own two feet and everything.

I leaned against the sliding glass door to the bedroom and did the slide thing again. This time the balcony tiles did the bum numbing but I had the view through the glass fence panels and managed to hold out a bit longer. I realised I couldn't spend my days wandering from door to door and sliding aimlessly down to lounge on the floor until hypothermia set in; it was going nowhere as far as a recovery strategy was concerned. Truthfully though, I didn't care and at that point in time I had no inkling there needed to be a strategy, or any kind of plan for the rest of my life. I couldn't even think far enough forward to my next meal. I wasn't 'dysfunctional', I was just not functioning at all. Dysfunction means you are functioning but not properly. I wasn't doing anything and I had no concerns about this whatsoever. Ever felt that way?

One day everything is weighing you down. The pressure is palpable, you can feel it like a real weight on your chest or shoulders. Then there are the numb bum days. You feel nothing. You have no awareness of any commitments, appointments, things you have to do, nothing. You just exist from breath to breath and it's a good thing that is handled sub-consciously or automatically or whatever because if you had to tell yourself to breathe you wouldn't bother. Do you know what I mean?

It was a Friday. Dad and Mum were flying out in a week, or ten days, I lost track. I just sat in the banana lounge on the balcony and thought how wonderful it would be if I could go with them. Me and Laura. Me, Mum, Dad, Laura, Billy. The five of us off together on an adventure. Far from the maddening crowd. Off to England for the summer, or maybe Spain. No Stewart, no Nathan, no Marg, none of them. Just us. I sat there for two or three hours. It was dark when I finally snapped out of whatever it was I was in and went and put the kettle on for a coffee. I cranked up my iPad and did some online stuff; checking for emails, reading a few Facebook posts, the usual. Had one of those spam emails from some Nigerian prince who swore if I helped him escape he would pay me half of his millions inherited from his father who had been imprisoned and executed by the government. He looked rather dishy in the photo he included but I knew he was probably fat, old and ugly and this was some Nigerian pop star's photo. I'd fallen for one of these scams before, up to a point. We had swapped emails and within six emails and two days he was swearing how he was in love with me and how if I could just send him three hundred dollars he could get a passport and a visa and come and see me. Then he could access the millions his dad had left him etc. When I asked Dad how do I send money by Western Union to Nigeria, he had gone ballistic. That was when I learned a valuable lesson about how easy it can be to get scammed, especially if you are emotionally vulnerable at the time.

As I erased the spam email from the latest Nigerian prince of my dreams I had one of those light-bulb moments. I swear, a light bulb came on above my head. Passport! If I had a passport for Laura I could go with Mum and Dad and Billy to England, or Spain, anywhere. I realised I didn't even know where Laura was being kept from me by Stewart, but while I looked for her I could arrange the passport, have it ready for when I did find her. I googled 'passport application for baby' and started doing the research.

"Mary, yes, it's Sarah. How can I…what can I do for you?" I was stunned, to be honest. Mary had called me at work the Monday after I moved into my new flat. I was immediately on my guard because I figured Stewart had put her up to finding out where I had moved to. He knew the old flat was now let to some other tenants and all his stuff and mine was gone. I had his stuff in a big crate at the factory and all my things were in the new flat, most of them waiting to be unpacked.

"Well, I, er, I , well, I… Look, whatever is going on between you and Stewart, well, I just want to say that I'm not taking sides. No, honestly. I know he's my son and all but… well he's too much like his father and so, well, I just wanted you to know that I understand how it has been for you, really, I do."

I was even more stunned now! "Mary, er, well, thanks, I, er I mean I, well, thanks." I sounded like some kind of idiot but really, this was a turn up for the books.

"Look, I am Laura's grandmother and I know how your mum and dad must feel, not being allowed to see their granddaughter. It's not fair so I thought we might arrange something between ourselves."

"What did you have in mind, Mary?" I was confused. Part of me wanted to ask right away where was my baby; another part screamed 'play it cool!', 'don't blow it!'. Mary would know where Stewart was living and keeping Laura. I was hesitant to come right out and ask but Mary saved me the trouble.

"Laura is with Stewart, and Stewart is staying with his dad and that woman." The way she said 'that woman' filled me with hope. Maybe she was more Marg's enemy than my friend, but right now I didn't care. I would ally myself to anyone that would get Laura into my hands. Maybe long enough to get her to the airport and on the first plane to Heathrow. "I have no idea where they are but I get to see Laura every Friday and Monday. In fact, she's here right now."

My heart stopped. I opened my mouth but no sound came out, not even a croak, or a squeak or a mumble. Nothing. I was so caught up with my emotions I just burst into tears."

"Sarah, don't cry." Those three words were spoken with such sincerity. The kind of empathy only someone who had suffered could say them like that and only someone suffering could appreciate the emotion within them.

"I just want my baby back."

"Well, I can't give you the baby; Stewart says he has legal custody and there is a court order… but he didn't say you can't see your baby. Not legally anyway. I mean there is no legal reason you can't see her, it's just him and that bitch Marg playing their games. Do you want to see Laura, Sarah?"

I cried yes, yes, YES! I sobbed and sniffed and moaned yes. Mary let me wind down before she told me where to meet her and Laura. She said my parents could come too but I had to swear we wouldn't try and take Laura. If I did the police would take her back and Mary would never be allowed to let me see my baby again. I swore I would not do anything stupid, I just wanted to hold my baby. It had been two months at least, I'd lost track but I knew it was too long. I called Mum as I ran for my car and told her where to meet me, a Starbucks not far from the factory. She said she would be there with Dad as soon as they could get there.

***

They were the best two hours of my life I had spent in the past year, if not forever. I had my Laura and she was beautiful. I didn't want to let her go, even to let Mum and Dad have a nurse, but I did. Mary was wonderful, just like Stewart at his nicest, you could see where he got the nice side of his character from. It was as different as chalk and cheese to the nasty, Nathan side. The side Marg found so easy to manipulate. Mary opened up more while we were there, at least once Mum and Dad arrived. I think she knew what they had been going through, they were the same age and everything.

I had taken a photo of Laura on my iPhone, head and shoulders on a pale background, just as the directions on the passport application web page insisted on. I had the passport application form in front of me. I downloaded it from the same web site, printed it off and filled it out. Now I was at the tricky part. I needed a witness to sign and say they knew me and knew Laura and they were able to recognize my signature and that of Stewart. They were the witness to the authenticity of the application, in other words. I needed someone I could trust but whoever I asked, they would be an accessory to a criminal offence. Making a false passport application or falsifying the signature of someone for the purposes of obtaining a passport was a Federal offence. Who could I ask to do that?

Let me explain. I had made a vow this afternoon while my baby slept in my arms for the first time since I was admitted to the hospital. That vow was that I would find a way, no matter what it took, to get my daughter away from her father and into my care. The best way to do this and make it stick would be to get Laura out of the country. Get her to the UK. To do this I needed two things. First of all I need Laura and until today that had seemed the hard thing. Now, with a second visit agreed for Friday, it was the easier of the two. The other thing I needed was a passport for Laura. I had the form, the photograph and I had read how I can apply for an emergency issue and get it in a couple of days. My plan was to drop in the application tomorrow and pick up the passport two days later. Then I would book two seats on the same flight to London as Mum and Dad. On Friday I would meet Mary, grab Laura and just walk out of the Starbucks she had set as the meeting place again; what could she do to stop me in a public place? I would get my bags out of my car and just leave it in the Starbucks car park, grab a cab to the airport with Laura and fly away.

The timing would be critical but Dad had taught me well, I was confident I could pull this off. It was the passport application that was holding me back. I needed someone to sign as witness. Someone who knew Laura, knew me and knew Stewart and was willing to risk a criminal conviction to help me. I couldn't ask Mum or Dad, besides they were ineligible as they were relatives. I couldn't ask Mary for the same reason, although she would probably not agree anyway. She might not like Nathan or Marg, but Stewart was her son and Laura her granddaughter and I was about to take her away from her. No, there had to be someone else.

It is not until you need someone desperately that you realise how few real friends you have. People you can trust with, if not your life then at least your future, which in time is the same thing. I had no one. Absolutely nobody I could ask to do such a thing. I didn't want my friends to get into serious trouble, especially not after I had flown away and was safe overseas. They extradite you from England but not from Spain and I could always take Laura to Mum and Dad's villa on the 'Costa Fortune', or wherever it was. I had no one I could trust among my friends, no one I was willing to put in such a position; but then it dawned on me. Why not use one of Stewart' friends? One who wouldn't bother to ring up and check and who didn't see him often enough to be able to let the cat out of the bag in three or four days. One who would do it for something in return that obligated him to keep his mouth shut. I thought of the mates Stewart went to the pub with but everyone of them would want sex with me as the payment and I wasn't that desperate just yet. Then it hit me. Shane! Shane would sign the form and he only spoke to Stewart if Stewart called him. In fact, if I recalled rightly, they had had a falling out over something or other to do with the Commodore, so Shane wouldn't be rushing to tell Stewart anything. He would twig that I was going to take Laura away from Stewart but that wouldn't bother him. Especially not if he got something in return. Something valuable; like my car.

Dad had helped me buy a new car after the debacle of the last one, which was something else I could use as leverage with Shane. It was a two year old Toyota Yaris, worth ten or twelve grand all day. If Shane signed the application and kept his mouth shut, providing I got the passport approved, I would let him have the car and sign over the rego papers so it was all legit. It was nearly midnight when I called him to talk about it but he agreed readily enough. I left out the bit about it being a federal offence, I figured he either already knew the law better than me or it wouldn't make any difference to him anyway. I went round to see him right then and there; he wanted to check out my Toyota before he would agree, but he liked what he saw and signed the back of the photo, the form and a letter I wrote up letting him have ownership of the car if it all went to plan. It was three in the morning by the time I went to bed and I had to be up early for the trip to the passport office in town, but I was happy. Maybe the happiest I had been since holding Laura just twelve hours earlier. How my life had turned around in just those twelve hours.

Boldness Be My Friend

I remember when I was eleven or twelve reading an old book about some men in World War Two escaping from a POW camp. It was a children's edition but still pretty scary. I always wondered if I would have the courage to do what the men in the story did. Would I have the guts? Would I seize the day? Would I ask boldness to be my friend? Teenage girls don't get much opportunity to challenge themselves with life or death, all or nothing decisions and even in my twenties it didn't seem like I was going to have to screw up my courage and make a big leap of faith or do something that might end up in disaster, or success.

I think women in general aren't really considered hero material, or heroine to be specific. We just get sidelined like women's sporting teams. They might play soccer or hockey or cricket as well as any men's team but who wants to watch? Who wants to pay to watch is more the real argument. Once a woman gets pregnant she is pigeon-holed and put away as being of little use out of the bedroom, kitchen, laundry or nursery for the next twenty years and by then she's too old, too ugly and too close to menopause to give a fair go to. At least that's how it seems to me.

You can imagine, then, the mix of emotions I was experiencing that Friday. I was scared but I was excited, anxious but impatient because as much as I feared failure, I wanted to get it done. Get it over with. I wanted to be on that plane with Laura and Mum, Dad and Billy and feel the plane push back from the gate, knowing the cabins doors were locked and armed and cross-checked I could pretend to pay attention to the safety briefing. I had dreamt of that moment, only to have the plane stop and go back to the gate and police come on board and take Laura away. Every cop looked like Stewart or Nathan and the cabin attendant was Marg with hideous make-up and a wicked laugh.

I put all those thoughts to the back of my mind and focused on the passport in my hand. I had picked it up yesterday as they had promised. Applied Tuesday, supplied Thursday. Yesssssss! I even pumped the air with the hand that didn't hold the passport. Laura's little face stared back at me as I read the details all over again. I had the passport, I had the ticket, I had everything but Laura. Shane was going to collect my car from the airport car park after I walked out of Starbucks with Laura. I would lock the keys in the boot, he had a spare set I dropped off yesterday after I picked up the passport. One less thing to worry about. I would lock the flat and leave it as it was. I didn't think about my stuff I left behind, everything I wanted in the world was waiting for me at Starbucks or in the two bags in the boot of my car. I never spared a moment's thought for Mum or Dad, or how they would manage the lease on the place without me paying the rent or moving my stuff out so someone else could take it over. I never gave any of these details any thought whatsoever because I was only thinking about Laura and getting her away, out of the country. I really hadn't thought anything through much at all past getting on that plane. If I had I might have foreseen some of the problems that could arise, but then maybe I would have changed my mind, missed my one and only chance. Boldness, be my friend. If ever I need a friend like you then this is the time!

I picked up the passports, tickets and my handbag and headed for the door. I caught a glimpse of myself in the hall mirror; slim, dressed casually, comfortably but stylishly in tailored cargo pants, comfy blouse and with my hair tied back, comfy runners with ankle socks. Just like Ashley Judd in that movie where she's a former spy hunting the kidnappers of her son. As I locked up I had a flash of clarity of thought and I knew if anyone could read my mind right at that moment they would think I was out of my depth. I wasn't Ashley Judd, not even the character she played according to a script a writer devised and a director explained. I was writing my own script, directing my own destiny and for a brief second or two, reality bit. I stood there, one hand still holding the door knob. I could unlock the door, go back into my flat and forget about the plan. I could leave the passports and tickets behind and just see Laura. Maybe we could make it a regular thing, every Monday and Friday at Starbucks?

I didn't want a regular thing twice a week at a coffee shop. I didn't want to see my daughter grow up between mocha lattes and flat whites. I wanted to be a mother. A parent. I wanted to be one of two parents, but if Stewart only wanted to paly games and make me suffer then I had to fight back. I had to take this chance. Maybe the only chance I would get. I had to do this, to summon up all of my courage and to try, at the very least try. Better to try and fail than to roll over and surrender without a fight.

I pulled the door closed and locked it, pocketed the key and turned to head for the lift. I was determined to do this, to carry out my plan. A bold and cunning plan as Dad was fond of saying. Why not? What did I have to lose? I thought then I had lost everything they could take from me anyway but I was wrong. I was soon to find out just how wrong I was.

***

"Sarah! Sarah don't! Don't do this!" Mary was distraught. She was following me to the door of Starbucks, not quite stopping me but clearly not letting me leave without registering her disapproval. Mum and Dad were still sitting at the table, looks of total astonishment on their faces. I had just announced my plan to take Laura with me. I didn't say anything about having a passport for her or leaving the country with them. Just that Laura was going with me.

"Mary, I'm sorry. Really I am. Truly. But you understand, surely? I can't…"

"Sarah don't do this. Not like this. Stewart will win this way. He'll get custody permanently and you will be declared an unfit mother and mentally incapable. You can't win like this!"

She didn't know I could win, I would win. She didn't know I had the passport and the tickets and I was heading for the airport. By now we were in the carpark and I was strapping Laura into the baby capsule I had bought yesterday. I could have taken the one Mary brought Laura in but I wanted a smooth exit. Just stand up and walk out. I wanted to wait while Mary went to the toilet but she didn't go and I was running out of time. I had to be at the airport three hours before departure for international flights. I figured I could shave that down to two hours if necessary, holding a baby and everything. I didn't want to be spending too much time on the wrong side of the immigration barrier in case Stewart headed for the airport to take Laura back. I wasn't sure how he would know to do this or if he would have the time, but I wasn't taking any chances. I'd just stood up and walked off without a word to Mum or Dad on purpose too. I wanted it to be as much a surprise for them as Mary. Maybe that would stop Mary thinking they were in on it and I was taking Laura to England with them.

"I'll see you when you come back, OK Mum?" I said that twice, just wanted to make sure Mary picked up on the fact I wasn't leaving.

"What? What are you doing, Sarah?"

"Sarah, don't be bloody stupid!" Dad was quicker on the uptake than Mum this time. "You can't just take her. Mary says Stewart has a court order for custody. You take her and you are breaking the law. They can lock you away!"

He really sounded worried, almost frantic, but I figured he just didn't want any more drama before they left. I just stood up and walked out. They were in the car park too, now. Mum was holding Billy and Dad was coming over to the car. Mary was crying. I felt sorry for her. I had betrayed her I know, but what could I do? I had to choose between her and Laura and of course, my daughter won.

"Sarah, love. Don't do this. Come back inside."

"I love you Dad. I love you Mum. Don't worry, Mary, I won't do anything stupid. Laura is perfectly safe. I won't harm her. Look, I gotta go." And that was that. I shut the car door, started the engine and drove off. I looked back in the rear view mirror and saw the three of them standing there, mouths wide open but nobody saying a word. I nearly feinted with the rush of adrenalin I had been bottling up since I made the decision to stand and walk out. I had butterflies in my stomach and an icy cold, sweet taste in my mouth and my head was spinning. I pulled myself together so I could drive safely; no point getting away with Laura only to put us both in the hospital or a cemetery.

At the airport I parked the car as agreed with Shane, left the keys in the boot and walked off with Laura and the two suitcases on a trolley someone had abandoned in the space next to mine. By the time I had found the right check-in counter Mum and Dad had arrived and were about five people behind me in the queue. I couldn't help smiling like some kind of blithering idiot.

"Sarah! What the…!"

"Sarah, Laura, I don't believe it!"

Believe it, Mum. We're going to England with you. If that's alright?"

I left my spot in the line and moved back to stand with Mum and Dad. No doubt the people between us were happy they were one check-in closer to the Duty Free shopping. Dad took Laura off my hands and played with her while I explained how I'd planned the whole thing and then carried it out. I know they were both shocked but also proud of me for having the guts to go for it. Still, they couldn't help themselves being parents and old and everything.

"Sarah, if you are caught with a passport obtained through false declarations and signatures, well, that could mean prison time. Seriously, pet, this is serious!" Dad was repeating himself and Mum wasn't correcting him so I knew they were deeply concerned but to be honest, I didn't care. All I cared was that it had worked. I had won. I had Laura and her passport and we were about to check-in and then board the plane and fly away.

"I'm sorry, Miss Clarkson. There is a no-fly order placed on your daughter."

"A what?"

"I beg your pardon," Dad jumped in. "What do you mean a 'no-fly order'?"

"Precisely that. The holder of that passport is not allowed to fly. They can't leave the country."

"How's that possible?"

"Someone has applied for a no-fly restriction to be made on the child. Do you have the permission of the father to take the child out of Australia, Miss Clarkson?"

"Yes, of course she does!" Good on you Mum! Mum had jumped in and was echoed by Dad saying the same thing.

"We're the grandparents, see, Clarkson, same name," Dad showed the check-in clerk his passport. "This is a family trip, to the UK. To see relatives. This is our son, same age as Laura but…"

"I understand Mr Clarkson but none of that makes any difference. The child cannot leave the country. I can not check her in or issue a boarding pass. If I did I would be guilty of a crime and the airline would be fined a huge amount and besides, you wouldn't get past immigration."

I couldn't believe it. All my planning wasted. How did he know? How could he have put a no-fly order on Laura's passport so quickly? I only signed for it yesterday afternoon, less than twenty four hours ago. I was just standing there, so close to crying, holding Laura, not knowing what to do.

Dad was talking to the clerk again, asking lots of questions I just didn't comprehend. I wasn't following anything at that moment, just too shocked and, well defeated. So close! So close but no boarding pass. I couldn't handle it and I just sat down on the floor, right there at the check-in counter. No door to slide down this time, I just dropped. I was half perched on one of the bags. I remember feeling it being dragged from under me and I was plopped on the tiles. Why is it always cold tiles I end up sitting on?

'C'mon, love, get up. Let's go." It was Dad. He had some boarding passes in his hand, my bags were gone and we just stood there holding two babies and some carry-on luggage. "Let's get a coffee."

We walked over to the coffee shop next to the departure gate. I sat down staring at all the people leaving Australia, standing at the gate, getting their photo taken, waving to loved ones, everyone happily crying away. Mum went and bought the coffees while I sat there. Laura needed a feed so I took out a bottle I had prepared earlier and started to give it to her. Dad looked on, a strange smile forming at the corners of his mouth.

"You look just like your mum when she had you. Dead spit."

I didn't answer, just sat there holding the baby in one arm and the bottle with the other. I was crying now. Not loud, racking sobs. They would come later. Sobs. Seeping out of my soul type sobs. Sniffs. Sobs, sniffs and pain. I could feel my heart ripping away from my ribs and tearing itself in two. I knew sooner or later some policeman or woman would come and take Laura out of my arms and put the handcuffs on me and I would never see her again. Ever.

"Sarah. SARAH!" Dad was shaking my bottle arm. "Sarah, did you hear what I said?" No, I hadn't heard anything except my heartbeat stopping and Laura's fading away to nothing. Little bump-bump noises. Bump-bump. Bump-bump. Bump-bump.

"Sarah, your dad is right. It's for the best, love." Mum was agreeing with Dad about something. But what I had no idea. I had tuned out totally.

"What? What did you say, Dad?"

"I will stay here with Laura. Give her back to Stewart. You and Mum and Billy board the plane and I will catch up with you tomorrow in Singapore. We had the stop-over booked anyway. Then we all fly to England and let the dust settle while we sort this out."

"But... the police. Won't they...?'

"What? No, they won't be doing anything just yet. Only if they check the passport details, which they will do eventually because the no-fly order has been activated and so they will follow it up. They are very strict on anything to do with kids leaving the country with only one parent. So far there has not been an offence. We complied with the no-fly order and Laura will not fly. She will remain here. We have to give her back to Stewart because he has legal custody. He placed that no-fly order on her name months ago. Back when you were in hospital as a matter of fact."

"What? How do you know this?"

"The clerk at the check-in showed me. Wasn't supposed to but I, er..."

"Your dad can charm the pants off a tailor's dummy, pet," Mum chipped in.

"Yeah, well, anyway, it seems the no-fly was imposed when Stewart got legal custody due to 'mental incapacitation of mother'. I saw it written there on the screen! No mention of it being temporary or you getting better."

"That's the kind of thing that follows you forever, love. Haunts you."

"Yeah, well, we'll beat it, love, don't you worry." Dad said that to Mum as much as to me. I wondered if he believed it as much as he meant it? I know how people feel about people who have a mental illness, no matter what kind or how mild. Once the word 'mental' is thrown in you've had it. We talked about that in my therapy sessions at the hospital.

So that was that. I had failed. Doomed to fail before I even began. If I had known he had imposed a no-fly order I would never have even tried to get a passport. Never have forged his signature or done the deal with Shane to be witness and take my car. I had lost my car, my kid, my clean no-criminal record. I was screwed, right royally. He had won. Again. The bastard. Now I was going to go running off to England with my parents and baby brother. Leave Laura to Stewart and his twisted father and evil step-mother and never see her again. If I set foot back in Australia I would be banged up forever. At least these were the thoughts going through my head as I nursed Laura for the last time. They were calling for boarding of our flight and we still had to get through immigration and all the way to the departure lounge but I couldn't let Laura ago. I just hung on to her and cried.

Mum pried her away and gave her ever so gently into Dad's arms. He was standing there almost crying himself as we walked through the departure gate and headed for the immigration counters. I can barely remember what happened after that. From the immigration counter to the moment the plane began to push back from the airbridge was a blur. Mum said later she was so worried the security people would think she was on drugs and stop us and we'd miss the plane. We were the second last ones to board, only a minute behind the usual last minute shopper who always seems to hold everyone else up while they day dream through duty-free.

As the cabin attendant began to point out the exits I seemed to snap out of my daze and I just sat there, stiff as a board. Then I crumpled, slid as far down as the seat and seat belt allowed, leaned against the window and cried my way to Singapore.

Part Six – Adam

Come And Get Her, Copper

I couldn't believe it when I saw Sarah and Laura at the airport, just a few people ahead of us at check-in. If I had been gob-smacked when she walked out of Starbucks with Laura, seeing her now was like getting a boot to the goolies. My mind was racing with all the possibilities, probabilities and potential crap that could come thundering down from a great height because of this. I had checked with the court and Stewart was the declared legal guardian of Laura. He did have custody and he could allow or deny her access and visitation. Unless she went to court and had the court change whatever arrangements Stewart may have allowed, he was running the show.

I have to admit the no-fly order was a stroke of omniscient genius. But how did he know Sarah might try to take Laura overseas? He wasn't that bright, our Stewart. He was firing the bullets but someone else was loading the rifle. I knew straight away who it was. Not that idiot of a bogan father of his. No, he could barely remember to tie his shoe laces. No, this was her work. Marg. Cunning as a shit house rat and as arrogant as the big one with the gold tooth. I had trusted her, once. Totally. With my business, with everything. Not all at once but over the years I had been given no reason not to trust her more and more and, I confess, it was convenient. We all take the path of least resistance and do more to avoid pain than gain pleasure. Letting Marg get on with things meant Sue and I could enjoy our hard work, or the fruits of it anyway.

Marg had systematically set about ripping off the business for as much as she could. Hundreds of thousands of dollars embezzled from our turnover. To think of the times when I was kept awake worrying about how we were going to make the wages bill on Friday and she had already stolen more than enough to pay the men for the whole year. The bitch! I kicked myself for letting it go on, for not picking up the signs and for not seeing what, it now seems, so many of the lads already knew. I was pissed off with them for not telling me but in all fairness it wasn't their job and if they suspected her but had no real proof, they would have been the ones to go for the high jump. It's a bit hard for the boys in the field to prove the money is going when they can't see the original orders and compare them with what they are handling on the job. Nah, not their fault. I'm the captain of this ship, the buck stops here.

I had picked up my granddaughter and my carry-on bag and her bag of bottles, nappies and whatever else she needed and headed for the office the check-in clerk had told me I had to report to with the baby before I could leave the airport. I figured the procedure was the check-in people would report the execution of the no-fly to immigration and the Federal Police, maybe the State Police, too. Someone would get the word to Stewart and he would come and collect Laura. I wasn't sure how long I would have to wait but I figured it would be a while. It was.

I sat in this bare, no, it was more stark than bare, stark room for five hours. I was given two cups of water that were coloured brown and claimed to contain coffee and milk with some sugar. I was allowed to visit the toilet while a woman in a customs and immigration uniform gave Laura a cuddle. I was allowed to sit there and stare at the walls and read the same three boring government printed posters warning about not properly declaring food stuffs or visits to areas with yellow fever. I fell asleep, then woke up in time to give Laura another feed, change her nappy and hand over a clean, burped and sleeping baby to her father.

"Where's Sarah?"

No 'hello Adam, how are you'. Not even a reach for his daughter. He just stepped into the room and stood there asking where Sarah was. No doubt he was hoping she was next door and he would have a chance to gloat. Remind her once more of how he had won, how he was in control, how he had the power. I felt like powering a fist into his snot locker but I knew that would get me nowhere. I wasn't bothered about the cops or anything, more that I knew antagonizing this little turd wasn't going to win me anything other than more petty bullshit. I'd had enough petty bullshit to last me another lifetime so I figured my best bet was to be amicable and as neutral as possible. Without betraying my blood or bowing to this piece of excrement. I had to be as diplomatic as I could and diplomacy has never been my strong suit.

"She's left the country. Gone back to the UK." I thought if he knew she was out of the country and out of his life, for now, he might ease up and I could get something from it. Maybe he'd agree to talk to Sarah, or let her see the baby when she came back, something.

"Good riddance. Bloody nutcase, that bitch."

"Hey! She's my daughter, remember?" I said it far more harshly than I had intended but screw him.

"Yeah, well, she's fucked up this time. Big time, this time." He laughed at his childish non-rhyme.

"Look, Stewart. You have Laura." Actually, he didn't. She was still in my arms and he hadn't made a move to take her from me. I knew then and there just what she really meant to him. A pawn. A tool. A weapon. Something to use to lord it over someone else. That was all he was, when you boiled it right down. A bully. A shitty little bully. A nothing character who only had any value or even self-esteem when he was being a prat and a prick. "Take her, here." I offered Laura to her father and he half stepped forward, then came up and took her. He was gentle, but in that too gentle way those unfamiliar with holding babies often are. I figured most of the care Laura got at his place was from Marg or Mary. I nearly took her back right then and there. I was torn between doing the right thing by my granddaughter and the right thing by the law.

In the movies the character playing me would have said damn the law, the law is an ass and punched the character playing Stewart in the mouth and walked out with the baby. Pull back as he walks towards a distant light source, music begins, credits roll, everyone cheers and that's all folks. In the movies. But this wasn't a movie. This was real life and in real life you don't smack people in the gob, no matter how much they deserve it. You also don't walk off with your granddaughter into the sunset without the police arresting you and handing the baby over to community services and you going to court and spending a fortune to stay out of jail and maybe spending a few months in jail regardless, and your business goes bankrupt and your family splits up from the pressure and that is that. That's real life. That's what happens to real people, not that movie make-believe shit people like to think happens.

"This is the way the world ends, not with a bang but a whimper.' That was a poem I had to read and memorise at school called 'The Hollow Men' by T.S. Eliot. I can't remember the rest, just that last line but that's enough. I felt like a hollow man. I had to cop the shit this little prick was spouting about my daughter, about me, my family. I had to keep my mouth shut and my hands to myself because I know what real life means. It means you can't punch whoever you like, no matter how much they deserve it. You can't just take your baby and bring her up in love and the way she should be brought up because the law says the other parent has rights. Screw the rights of the kid or the grand parents or the other parent. If one parent works the system, their rights are more righteous than anyone else's it seems. All animals are created equal but some are more equal than others. I read that at school, too. Animal Farm by George Orwell. So bloody true. Here was the worst animal on the farm laughing and lording it over us because they twisted the law to their own ends first. They beat us to it, regardless of the fact we wouldn't have done what he did. Stupid us would have played the game fair. Given him a fair go and done the decent thing. Done unto others as we would want done to us. Screw that! From now on, from that moment in that bare room when Stewart stood there and laughed at me and my family; that's when I swore I would play the game differently. Not their way. Not the right way. Not the legal way. From now on I would play it my way. My way. Me. I was playing to win and sod anyone else.

"Tell Sarah not to bother begging. She won't see Laura ever again if I get my way."

Stewart had grabbed the bag of baby things and was half out the door. The customs officer was looking away, I could tell she was as disgusted at his behaviour as I was. I could have said something. I could have said a lot of things but the only things I wanted to say right then and there were not the kind of things you say in front of a witness. I knew it would only come back and bite me on the arse later.

"Look after her, Stewart. Laura, I mean. Try and do a better job with her than you did with Sarah." At that I turned around and busied myself with my carry on bag, my empty paper coffee cup, anything to not turn around and snot the little bastard. I heard him hesitate, mumble something and then he was gone. Didn't even bother to close the door behind him. I looked across at the customs officer. She looked away and headed for the door saying I was free to leave and that was that.

I had originally planned to grab a room at the airport motel just across from the terminal, but Sarah had left some things behind she wanted now and so I had said I'd spend the night there and bring them with me the next day. As she handed over her front door keys I noticed the car keys were not on the ring but I said nothing. I would learn later, when we were on the way to Heathrow, what had happened to her car and the deal she had made to get that passport for Laura.

Letting myself in to her apartment, I saw myself reflected in the full length mirror that ran the length of the hall. I thought it was my father standing there, I looked like an old man. I realised I was about the age my dad was when he died from cancer. I just stood there for a minute or two, then closed the door behind me and went and sat down on the couch.

I made a cup of decent coffee and sipped it slowly while I tried to piece together the events of the past few days. It had all been a blur in so many ways. Moving Sarah into the flat had been like a weight was taken off our shoulders. Sue and I were relieved we had our home back, without the drama and drudgery of Sarah and her problems to take over our lives. I know it sounds like we are selfish but you try and live someone else's life for them? Especially when they made choices there is no way you would have made. Choices you warned them would turn out badly. Then you have to suffer, because you do suffer. Anyone with a family member suffering depression of any form knows everyone suffers somehow, to some degree. We had suffered for months. A year nearly. It was time to say enough is enough and to take action to fix things. If we couldn't fix Sarah's problems, at least we could make sure they weren't our problems, too. I mean, she's a grown woman, an adult. She made her bed and no matter how untidy or uncomfortable, she is the one that has to lie in it.

Which is all very true but it doesn't stop you from feeling bad when you do take action and sort things out. That is the price you pay, I guess. It was that thought, the bit about paying a price, that switched my thoughts over to my problems. My business and more specifically, the woman who had ripped me off for maybe half a million dollars. I wasn't going to run off to England and leave that still floating around. Her laughing she had run me out of the country and kept hold of my money. I knew where she lived. Why not go there, knock on her door and demand she pay back every cent! Why not? I couldn't think of a single reason so I called a cab and did just that.

Mind The Step

The house Marg had rented was what is known as a 'Queenslander'. Made of timber with a corrugated iron roof, raised up on stilts with a bull-nosed verandah running around the outside and stairs leading up from the street. Underneath there were boxes and an old sofa, a table and some garden chairs and a BBQ on wheels. A nice, six burner job, no doubt paid for with my money. Everything in the house, including the rent, was probably paid for with my money. There was a new Falcon sedan in the driveway, one of those high performance models, bright electric blue with black go-faster stripes and fat, low profile tyres. Again, my money at work. I asked the cab to wait, told him I'd only be a few minutes and gave him a fifty; getting another cab around here at night would be a hassle and I just wanted to say my piece and get the hell out of there.

I wasn't even sure what I was going to say. She'd deny everything, of course. I'd run through several dialogues in my head on the way over but the cabbie kept interrupting. Just my luck to get a talkative foreign student keen to practise his English. I walked to the stairs and paused. Was this a good idea? I really didn't know the answer to that. All I did know was my daughter and wife were in a hotel in Singapore by now, no doubt worried sick about Laura and maybe even me, whether I'd make it to them on the next day's flight or get stuck here. I'd told them to take the booked flight to London even if I was delayed; no point racking up three lots of charges to change bookings. Flying might be a lot cheaper these days, but the discount airlines charged for every little thing. I figured they'd even charge you for the oxygen if one of those masks dropped from the overhead compartment and you had to suck on it to stay conscious.

I decided I was here now so I had better get it over with. I couldn't bear the thought of someone seeing me slink back to the cab from one of the windows. There was an orange glow coming from behind the curtains, it seemed so homely and welcoming; not what I expected from the home of a thieving, lying, manipulating bitch. With that thought I climbed the stairs, nearly putting my foot through the third one that was almost rotted away. I had to catch hold of the railing to stop myself tripping over and ending up arse over head back on the street. I gingerly tested the next two steps but made it onto the verandah without further worry. There was a screen door in front of the main door, locked, and the type where those inside can see out but you can't see them. I had them on most of my properties and always thought they were a good idea, but then that was when I would have been the one looking out, not the one looking in. And wondering. What if Nathan answered the door with a shotgun? He had one; Marg told me he kept it beside the front door of their old place… just in case. I never asked 'just in case of what?' Just in case the boss you stole half a million bucks from turns up and asks for his money back, perhaps.

I had second thoughts again, or would that be third thoughts? This was seeming more and more like a bad idea with every bang of that drum I could hear. Then it dawned on me. The drum was my heart. I realised my hands were shaking and I could feel the butterflies breaking out of their cocoons in my stomach. I wasn't scared, just pumped. Pumped full of adrenalin. The response is the same, apparently. Whether you are scared or angry and ready to fight. Same signs and symptoms. The brain prepares the body for fight or flight. To survive. To run like hell or to fight like a cornered rat. Well Marg and Nathan were the rats, I just hoped they didn't feel too cornered. At least not enough to do anything stupid. I knocked.

My knock sounded loud enough to wake the street. It was after eleven by now and while I didn't expect anyone in this house to be tucked up in bed, I guess if someone banged on my door less than an hour the decent side of midnight I might be a little wary of opening it. I saw a chink of light appear to my right, someone was peering through the curtains onto the verandah. I snapped my head to one side to see who it was but they were gone in an eye blink. Oh well, the cat was out of the bag now so I banged on the door again. Louder.

I heard the locks being undone and then the door swung wide open and I could make out a dark shape behind the screen. "What the fuck you want?" It was Nathan.

"I want my money, that's what I want. I want the half a million…"

"Fuck off! Nobody took your money. Piss off or I'll piss you off!"

"I'm already pissed off, Nathan. Where's Marg? I want to talk to her."

"I said, fuck off!"

"And I said I want my money and I want to talk to Marg. Bring her here now or I'll…" That was a mistake. Never give an ultimatum, at least not when you have nothing to use if they fail to comply. And I had nothing.

"Or you'll what?" It was Marg. I couldn't see her but the dark shape had grown larger. It resembled nothing other than a large black blob with some light around the edges pushing past to get out of the house. "What do you want, Adam?"

"I want my money, Marg. I want the half a million you stole from me."

"What money? I stole nothing from you. Or anyone else. You better be careful what you say or I'll sue you for every cent you have!"

"We know, Marg. We know it all. We found the book, the bank account, the computer software. Everything."

"Bullshit!" That was Nathan.

"The cops have everything. They'll be here tomorrow so better you work something out with me now, than..." I was making this up as I went along. The police did have everything but they said they wouldn't be bringing Marg in for questioning until they had more evidence. Didn't want her slipping the net if they jumped too soon. I had a flash of inspiration if you can call it that. I realised I might have let the cat out of the bag and they'd pack up tonight and go on the run and the police might take years to find them. Bugger!

"So what? They can't prove anything." She didn't sound quite so sure of herself now. "We done nothing."

"I'm not arguing with you, Marg. I want my money. I don't care if you go to jail or not, just so long as I get my money back. Or as much as you've got left." I threw that in to try and salvage the conversation. Maybe if she saw a chance at staying out of prison she would return what she had left and make arrangements with me. Screw that of course. Soon as she coughed I would be jumping up and down for the judge to throw the book at her and put her away for twenty years.

"Piss off! She didn't take your stinking money. You think you are so good, so much better than anyone else, you think your money makes you a big man." Nathan was winding up, obviously he had a problem with anyone more successful than he was. Which was just about everyone in Australia.

"I don't have your money, Adam." Her tone had changed, subtly, it was a notch softer. I think she meant she didn't have it any more, that she had spent it all.

"All gone, Marg?"

"I don't have your money, Adam." Then she hardened up again. "Never had it, OK? Now piss off!"

"I want my money and I'm going to get it!" I was really angry at them now. How dare they? I had never taken a cent from anyone except as payment for hard work. Not one cent in my life. This woman, this pair of bogan mongrels took whatever they could and didn't give a damn who suffered so long as they got what they wanted. Well I was going to give them what they deserved!

"What you doing?"

"Who you phoning?"

I had stepped back from the door and was almost at the steps when I took out my mobile phone and hit 0 three times. It took four rings before a recording told me it was an offence to make false 000 calls and if it wasn't an emergency I should call the switchboard... For chrissakes! If it was an emergency I would be dead before I could tell anyone! Shit, this was an emergency! I had the two mongrels that had stolen half a million dollars from me, manipulated Stewart into denying Sarah her own kid, had her put in a looney bin and… I was not thinking straight but I snapped out of it as the phone spoke in my ear.

"Emergency, Fire, Police or Ambulance?"

"Police, please."

"You fucken' bastard!" this came from behind the screen door.

"Putting you through, please hold…"

"You bloody prick! I'll friggin' kill you ya cun.."

"Police, what is the emergency?"

"My name is Adam Clarkson, I am at the house of the woman who stole half a million dollars from my business and her partner is threatening to kill me."

"You bastard!" the screen door was flung open and there was Nathan, wearing a blue singlet and a pair of Y-fronts. He was snarling and spitting and was the most savage, angry looking animal I have ever seen in my life.

"Does he have a gun, sir?"

"Put the phone down or I'll fucking shoot ya!"

"Yes, he…" my voice cracked, went up an octave and I sounded like a prepubescent teenager as I said, "a shotgun. He's got a shot…" I never finished the word because at that moment Marg barged past Nathan and flung herself onto the verandah. As she did Nathan was spun to one side and the shotgun went off. The sound was deafening and so close I saw the flash from the muzzle at the same time as the bang pushed me back. The blast missed my face by millimetres, I could feel the hot gases sear my cheek. The shot took out a piece of the bullnose roofing, a dozen holes appearing in the wriggly tin and adding to the noise. I must have taken a step back without thinking and now I was falling backwards, my hands flailing at the air for something to grab hold of but I just kept going backwards. I hit the steps mid-way down and felt the wood splinter under me. I came to rest jammed into the stair frame and totally helpless. Above me loomed Nathan, his face still a mask of hatred. Marg appeared beside him and then everything went into slow motion.

My ear was ringing from the blast, my cheek stung and my back was sending slivers of pain up and down my legs. I could see Marg's mouth moving and her hand reaching for the barrel of the shotgun; Nathan brushing her away and bringing the weapon to bear on me. I looked down the barrel of that 12 gauge pump action shotgun and I swear I could see the round in the breech. I saw everyone of the dozen or so steel balls that at any beat of my heart would explode out of the muzzle and tear my chest in two.

Marg hit Nathan on the shoulder and the arm, knocking the gun away from a direct line of fire that would kill me in a single blast. I was too close to survive, I knew that. Even as I lay there, unable to move, I knew this was it. This was how I was going to die. Adam Clarkson, your life is over. I watched, growing calmer with each fraction of a second as my senses shut down whatever was not needed to survive. I smelt nothing, not the cloud of gunsmoke settling down in the still night air. Not the faeces that my bowels automatically evacuated, instinctively knowing my chances of survival were just that little bit higher if I didn't have a gutful of digested food to slow me down or cause infection. I could feel the warmth of the urine my bladder had released to make sure that was one less complication should I be injured there. I smelt none of this. I felt none of this. I no longer heard anything and all I could taste was the sickly, sweet, icy cold adrenalin drying my mouth, making it impossible to even shout out, to say what? To say NO!

My only sense was my sight and that had narrowed to a tunnel of reflected light between me and that shotgun. Everything around it was a blur, but the barrel of that gun was in sharp focus, almost magnified. My body was working perfectly, just as nature had intended, just as it had evolved over millions of years. I was ready. Ready to die because there was no way I could escape. No way I could get up and counter attack. I could do nothing but wait and I knew I wouldn't be waiting long.

The shotgun exploded a second time. I saw the flash, I barely recall hearing the bang even though it was hardly any further away than it had been the first time. The blast flew over my head. He missed! My focus shifted, beyond the barrel of the gun, along the stock and up the arm holding it and stopped at his face. Nathan seemed puzzled. He had a look of bewilderment on his face and one hand slowly raised from the stock of the shotgun to rest on his head, just above his left ear. A red stain began to spread through his fingers.

Just as if he was following the Director's instructions, Nathan pulled his hand away from his head and looked at his red hand. Blood. His blood. He put his hand back to his head, then pulled it away and stared at it again. It was still red, still blood stained but now the blood was all down the side of his face, his neck and chest. He put his hand back to his head, thrust the shotgun towards Marg and, as she grabbed it with both hands, he crumpled to the floor.

All of a sudden I could hear again. The ringing in my ears was still loud but I could hear Marg screaming. I could hear someone talking to me. I could feel their hands lifting me out of the stair frame and helping me sit up on the second stair. I looked up and it was the taxi driver. The young Indian economics student.

"What..?"

"It is all OK, yes. I fixed him for you, sir! All over now!"

I managed to stand up, grateful I was not too badly injured and that my spine was still intact and functioning. My ear rang, my face stung and I stank to high heaven but... I was alive. My saviour noticed the smell emanating from my lower regions and couldn't help take a half step backwards, but he didn't let go and I was able to climb the stairs, dodging the hole I had made on my way down. I stood on the verandah next to Marg. She was still holding the shotgun and looking down at Nathan. He was lying with his legs crossed under his body, his back arched over with his head resting on the blood stained decking. He was dead. Nobody would stay in that posture if they were alive. I gently reached over and took the shotgun from Marg and threw it into the low bushes that ran along the side of the property. The police could find it easily enough and I didn't want to look at it for another second. Marg sat down on the porch seat and just stared at Nathan, not saying a word, not crying a tear. Just sitting there, totally in shock.

The taxi driver was reaching for something beside Nathan's body. It was a wheel brace. He must have thrown it at Nathan and hit him over the ear with it. A bloody good throw! It could just as easily have made Nathan pull the trigger and kill me but instead, it saved my life.

"Thank you." I said to the taxi driver. "Thank you. You saved my..." was all I got out before I, too, crumpled and just sat there. I was shaking with relief and adrenalin and the sheer love of being alive. I don't know how long I sat there but the police say they attended the scene within six minutes of the shotgun discharge being recorded on the 000 call. It seemed like the longest six minutes of my life, but at least I was still alive and for that, I was humbly grateful. "You want a job, ever. You see me. OK?"

"Thank you sir, but I have a job. I drive a taxi, remember?"

"Fair enough, mate. But you never know, life has a nasty habit of playing silly games with all of us."

Epilogue

I never made the flight to Singapore the next day, no surprise there. I was able to fly out to London a week later, but told I would probably be required to return for the Coroner's hearing, which would be some months down the track. The police assured me there wouldn't be charges laid against the taxi driver as he had acted in defence of me. There had been two other witnesses, neighbours who had heard either the yelling or the first gunshot and then watched the events unfold like some reality TV show.

Marg was on remand over her part in the shooting but she'd probably get off that. While in custody they were proceeding with the embezzlement investigation and she'd get done for that for sure. The wheels of justice turn slowly so I knew I could have a month or two in the UK, then come back and try and get things going again. The factory would still make money, I had good people running the business for me so that wasn't a problem. The problem was Sarah. And Laura. And Stewart.

Meeting me at Heathrow, Sue and Sarah were all tears and sobs and barely calmer than they had been when I Skyped them in Singapore the night of the drama. If anything, Sarah was even more withdrawn and desperate than before. Desperate to see her Laura. Desperate to get back to Australia, get custody of her daughter and then… Well she didn't know what to do then but then would take care of itself, it always does. We just had to get to the 'then' and that is another story.

Soon to be released; 'Sarah's Turn', the second installment in this all-too-real life drama.
For more information, visit http://sarahschild.com.au or join us on Facebook at Www.facebook.com/sarahschildbook
For more information on co-Author Perry Gamsby, http://perrygamsby.net

4337034R00091

Printed in Germany
by Amazon Distribution
GmbH, Leipzig